PRAISE FOR LAURENCE SHAMES' NOVELS

RELATIVE HUMIDITY

LAURENCE SHAMES

To Marilyn
And in memory of our mothers, Joyce and Helen
Everyone loved everyone. It could drive a person crazy.

Happy families are all alike. Every unhappy family is unhappy in its own way—Leo Tolstoy

You ain't lyin', baby—Little Richard

1.

Now and then, not often, life offers up a perfect moment, a moment when everything just fits together, almost as if there was a plan, as if the world had been designed to be at least an occasional Paradise for those who took the trouble to notice its ingenious construction, as if life would be a calm and peaceful pleasure if that moment just went on and on.

But of course it never does.

Pete Amsterdam, world's most reluctant and in fact completely accidental private eye, was savoring such a moment just a few heartbeats before a worse than usual shitstorm came swirling up to shatter the frail illusion of serenity and order.

He was sitting in his hot tub, naked of course, in his small backyard in Key West, Florida. It was January. The temperature was eighty-one degrees under a faultless and shimmering sky, and this alone was enough to call forth gratitude and a bit of self-satisfaction in anyone who'd grown up in the gray and thankless winters of New Jersey and had had the moxie and the luck to get the hell out of there. The water in the tub was a hundred and two, making for just enough contrast so that Pete could experience over and over again the innocently sexy thrill of lifting his neck and shoulders clear of the water to feel a cooling tingle, then dropping them back below the surface before the tingle had become a chill.

There was a flute of iced, bone-dry Champagne resting on the hot tub's edge. Bubbles rose in the glass as beads of condensation trickled down the stem. Through the outdoor speakers came a Mozart string quartet. Palm fronds swayed in perfect sync with the music. The tempo matched the rise of bubbles and the fall of condensation. Every detail contributed its bit of beauty; everything was of a piece, in balance. Pete gave a languorous sigh as he lifted an arm from the tub, shook droplets from his hand, took a sip of wine, and basked in the completeness of the moment.

That was when he heard the unlocked screen door of his house screech open and slam shut, the ugly sounds slashing through the music like a sudden tearing of silk. The slam was followed by a gratingly off-tempo clicking of footsteps on his hardwood floor, footsteps that were hauntingly familiar in their jarring and just slightly asymmetric cadence, as if one leg was struggling to keep up with the other, shuffling or being half-dragged behind its more insistent partner. The foreboding steps grew louder—click, shuffle; click, shuffle—and then there came the groan and clatter of his backyard slider being violently yanked open, and into his backyard haven barged the last person in the world he expected to see just then, and one of the last he hoped to.

By reflex, he recoiled, and water sloshed over the edge of the hot tub. He put down his Champagne and blinked at the invader as she strode and shuffled ever closer, bracelets jangling, her lipstick smeared beyond the outline of her lips, her brittle blonde hair askew above rhinestoned sunglasses with upsweeping frames. He felt the adrenaline coursing through his veins, a vague dread washing over him as the humidity seemed suddenly to spike, and in a squeezed voice he managed finally to say, "Hi, Mom. What the hell are you doing here?"

From half a step away she took a very brief but unembarrassed glance at her naked son beneath his imperfect veil of roiled water. "Peter," she said—no one else called him that and he really didn't like it—"maybe you should put some pants on like most people on a weekday afternoon, then maybe we can talk about it."

2.

The day before, a new guy in town, not known by any of the regulars, had taken a nasty fall during a pickleball game on what had formerly been the tennis courts at Higgs Beach.

It happened on court six. This was not a coincidence, as court six was the worst court because some local knucklehead had stolen its windscreen from the fence on the side that faced the ocean. This was a problem because the prevailing breeze in Key West comes from the southeast across the gray-green waters of the Florida Straits, and the photogenic palms that line the beach are much too scrawny to block the flow as it creeps or roars across the shoreline and the narrow sandy roadway that separates the beach from the courts. So, absent a windscreen for court six, the wind continued to whistle and moan through the chain-link fence and to create zany distortions in the flight of the nearly weightless pickleball. These airborne zigs and zags and dips and flutters inserted an unwelcome randomness into the game and sometimes forced the players to make abrupt and ungainly adjustments, which occasionally led to injuries.

So court six was usually unoccupied unless courts one through five were taken. But season by season, almost week by week, it seemed like one through five were always taken, as pickleball was booming in Key West. The sport just had a lot going for it. It was easy to learn. It required no fancy gear. You seldom had to run more than two steps at a time. The tempo was quick and the games were brief, so that even the most annoying contest was over almost before it could register as annoying.

Most important, since it seemed that practically everyone who played the game had taken it up only yesterday, there seemed to be a universal understanding that everyone was welcome and should be encouraged—the old, the slow, the braced and bandaged, the doddering or goofy who never knew the score or whose turn it was to serve; the seriously out of shape or seriously hung-over; the sketchy types who wore stripes with plaids and who always needed to borrow paddles and sometimes played in flip-flops; the folks who'd had a couple of pops or a couple of tokes before even getting to the court and who carried a bottle of tequila and a tin of marijuana gummies in their gym bag.

So it was perfect for the Higgs Beach crowd, and the better courts were almost always taken, with an overflow of tourists and kibitzers sitting in the bleachers and waiting their turn.

But to get back to what happened on court six:

A motley foursome was in mid-game. The new guy who would shortly take a header had been randomly partnered with a bartender named Nell, who worked at a local dive called the Eclipse Saloon. Their opponents were Ralph, a retired dry-cleaner from Brockton, Massachusetts, and Poet, a sandy-haired trustifarian with a distracted manner and an arsenal of elaborate spins.

It had been a friendly game, but the score was close and the intensity was rising as both teams neared the finish line. Then, on a crucial point, Poet hit a looping slice to the new guy's backhand, and what happened next took on some of the paradoxical quality of a car crash. On the one hand, it seemed to happen in super slow motion, with an agonizingly gradual build-up to an inevitable disaster; and, on the other hand, it seemed to happen so fast that it was impossible to be sure about exactly how or why it had occurred, or the order in which the separate pieces of the incident had unfolded, or which element was the cause and which was the effect.

All that seemed certain was that Poet's looping shot got caught up by a gust of wind that had blasted through the unscreened fence and started twisting crazily—dipping, dropping, slipping away like a dream upon waking—and the new guy kept chasing it. At some point, his gaze abruptly lifted off the ball, though exactly why that happened would later become a topic of discussion. The sudden jerk of his head apparently caused him to lose his balance. His leg buckled and his feet splayed out. He gave an anguished yell that might have been son of a bitch. As he went down, there was a sharp, cracking noise, though people would later disagree as to the source of the grim sound and whether it had come before or after the new guy hit the ground.

In any case, he went down hard. The paddle flew out of his hand. He groaned. Nell walked over to him, bent down, and asked if he was okay. The new guy winced, grabbed his leg, and said he thought it was his Achilles. Ralph offered to help him stand up but the injured man preferred to stay right where he was. Poet said he probably needed x-rays. The new guy didn't argue. Nell took out her phone and called an ambulance. After a while, its approaching siren could be heard slicing through the more usual Key West racket of motor-scooters and jet-skis and blasting radios. Everyone said how sorry they were as the new guy was carted off on a stretcher.

After he was gone, Nell and Ralph and Poet walked off to the bleachers for a break and, as they sipped their beers, they were drawn into conversation by an old kibitzer who often sat in the shady part of the stands to watch the games and render his opinion on any topic whatsoever. The kibitzer's name was Bert. He seemed to know everybody, or all the regulars at least, and everyone knew him, even though, as far as anybody was aware, he never played. With his yellow-tinged white hair and crinkled, papery skin, he seemed to be too ancient even for pickleball, though his posture was still straight, with the squared shoulders of a self-respecting man, and the deep-set black eyes beside his banana nose still had a twinkle. He generally wore crisp linen shirts with piping and a monogram, and he always had a nervous chihuahua named Nacho—mainly a pair of enormous ears with a tiny dog attached—spinning around in his lap. Now he leaned in toward the players from court six and said in his gravelly voice with the gruff yet oddly soothing Brooklyn accent, "Boy, that was a helluva fall that guy took. What the hell happened?"

The others looked at each other, but no one seemed exactly

sure. Nell said, "Looked to me like he jerked his head 'cause he was afraid of running into someone on court five."

Ralph said, "Nah, I don't think that's how it was. He wasn't really that close to anybody."

Poet said, "Well, he was clearly puzzled by the spin."

"I guess he was," said Bert, "but people get puzzled alla time wit'out they fall down and need an ambulance. So I'll tell ya how it looked to me. Okay, I'm sittin' far away and all, and I'm not gonna tell ya I got twenty-twenty no more, but from here how it looked is that the guy's chasin' the ball, then he sees somethin' outa the corner of his eye, but only, like, for a fraction of a fraction, so he finds the ball again, but then he can't help goin' back for a second look, a longer look, at whatever or whoever caught his eye inna first place. And that's when his feet get all bollixed up and he starts to fall and yells out somethin' that I couldn't quite make out from here."

"What he yelled out," said Ralph, "was 'son of a bitch,' which is what I guess a lotta guys would yell out if their Achilles just popped."

"Except I don't think that's exactly what he said," Nell put in. "What I think he said is 'you son of a bitch.'"

"Ah," said Poet. "That changes everything. That extra syllable. It shifts the whole cadence, the rhythm."

Bert considered that a moment. To aid him in his contemplation, he rubbed the dog's head as if the dog's head was his own chin. The dog stopped spinning. That was the only time he didn't spin; when he was getting his head rubbed. The old man said, "Due respect, Poet, and pardon my French, but fuck the cadence. Let's think about what it really changes. What it would change would be that he ain't just screamin' out in pain or, as you might say, anguish, as any ordinary mortal would unnerstandably be inclined to do if some piece a his anatomy had just peeled off a bone, but rather that he's directly addressin' and even disparagin' the female parent of another person who let's say he doesn't care for or otherwise would rather not see. Which would explain why he couldn't help himself from goin' back for that second look, maybe hopin' against hope that he didn't really see the person he thought he saw, but by then he's lost his balance and he's goin' down."

The others took a moment to decipher Bert's tormented syntax, then Nell said, "Well, if there was someone there that he got so upset about seeing, who would that have been?"

Ralph said, "So who was on court five?"

But after the beer and the exercise and the time in the hot sun, no one could remember, which almost certainly meant that the foursome on the neighboring court—who had finished their game and drifted off by then—had been tourists, since tourists wafted through Key West in such numbers and with such utter interchangeability that locals tended not to waste their attention on noticing them. So Nell and Poet just shrugged.

"And another thing," Bert resumed. "That cracking sound. Was it before or after he went down?"

"I thought it was when his paddle hit the ground," said Ralph.

"I think it happened a beat sooner," Poet said. "And was way too loud to be just that."

Nell said, "A friend of mine once tore her Achilles playing tennis. Said it felt like she'd been shot. Sounded like it, too."

"Hm," said Bert. "Shot. That's innerestin'. Do we know for sure this poor bastard wasn't shot?"

"Wasn't any blood," Ralph pointed out.

Bert shrugged. "People miss sometimes. Trust me on that. I wouldn't be here otherwise."

The other three, wanting to believe the old man must be joking, came out with slightly nervous laughs. They finished their beers, then a court other than court six became available, so they grabbed a new fourth from the bleachers and went back out to play some more. That's just how it was, in pickleball as in life. People got hurt and everyone was sorry for them and even spent a few minutes mulling over what had happened, and then the games went on.

3.

"So it's about Gianni," said Pete's mother, whose name was Gertie.

By then, Pete had risen from the hot tub, toweled off, slipped into a bathing suit, and grabbed a second Champagne flute from the kitchen. Mother and son clinked glasses at a small table next to the pool. The pool was Key West-size, just long enough to swim three strokes in, just deep enough to get your ribcage wet. There were skyflower bushes around the pool and allamanda vines on the wooden fence behind it.

Pete said, "Johnny?"

"Not Johnny. Gianni." She stretched out the syllables, hoping to make them sound more Italian. "You remember. Gianni Calabro. From The Grotto. In Bloomfield Center. We used to go there all the time back when you were growing up."

"The pizza joint?"

"It is not a pizza joint," said Gertie, briefly taking off her rhinestoned sunglasses and raising a heavily penciled eyebrow for emphasis. "It is a fine dining establishment that also offers pizza."

"Pizza's all I ever got there."

"You were a child, Peter. Your Dad and I didn't have much money. When we went out to eat as a family, it was pizza. Or maybe burgers or Chinese. Combination platter. Almost always on a Sunday, right? Usually there'd be an argument about who wanted which. But anyway, now and then your Dad and I would have a date night, a splurge. We'd got a sitter—"

"Beverly Weinstein. I still remember her pimples," Pete put in.

"—and we'd go out late on a Friday or Saturday, and Gianni would make us veal chops that were as good as anything you could get in Manhattan. Smothered in sage. Pink near the bone, crispy at the edge. Delicious."

"Okay, so the guy could cook a veal chop. But you still haven't told me—"

"Why I'm here? I'll get to it, I'll get to it. But you do remember Gianni, right?" She picked up her glass with a hand full of showy rings that had somehow made it past her swollen knuckles.

Pete thought back three decades or so. "All I have is this sort of vague image of a big guy in an undershirt with pizza flour in his chest hair."

"He happens to be a very elegant man when he isn't working in the kitchen. Your father and I got to know him very well. Sometimes we went to shows and dinner together, nice places, fancy places, in the City. And then…and then, when your father got sick, Gianni was extremely kind, and we stayed in touch and, well, one thing led to another, and Gianni and I have become, I guess you'd say, very close. Extremely close."

Pete sipped some wine and tried to take this in. "Mom, are you telling me you're shacked up with the pizza man?"

"That's a rather crude way to put it, Peter. And I wish you'd stop calling him that."

"Okay, okay. The veal chop guy. But if it's the guy I remember, he's gotta be, like, twenty years younger than you."

"Seventeen," said Gertie, and she couldn't quite hold back a blush and an incongruously girlish smile. "But who cares? Age is just a number, right?"

"Right, sure, but it's getting to be a pretty big number. Plus, listen, no offense Mom, but after the hip replacement thing, you still don't walk exactly right. I mean, it's no big deal, probably hardly anyone else would notice, but you do limp a little bit."

Masking wounded vanity with a rather haughty tone, she said, "I get around just fine."

"Apparently. But look, Mom, I'm not trying to sound negative. I'm happy for you. I am. It's just that it's a little bit of a shock."

"What, you don't think men find me attractive anymore?"

"Mom, you're my mother. I have no idea if men find you attractive or not. I've never really thought about it. Frankly, I think if I did think about it, it would be a little weird and Freudian and I'd probably need years of therapy to work it through. But in the meantime, what I still don't understand—"

She finished the sentence for him, as he somehow knew she would. "Is why I suddenly showed up here? S'okay, here it is. Gianni bought a place down here last month. Just a little condo. Plans to be a snowbird. I was hoping to come down for a visit after he was settled in, after he got his furniture, which of course he didn't get yet because the supply chain is still messed up. If it went like we were planning, I would've given you some notice. It would've been relaxed. But now it's more like an emergency. He seems to be in trouble, Peter. Maybe bad trouble, I can't tell."

Not really wanting to know more, Pete still couldn't hold back from asking what kind of trouble.

"Well, like, you know, the restaurant business, his connections in the City…"

"Mom, where we goin' with this?"

"Oh, come on, Peter, don't be naive. The quality of those veal chops? Two exits from where Tony Soprano lived?"

"Mom, are you telling you've become a Mafia moll at this stage of the game?"

Although it was just the two of them in the backyard, and even though Key West's background hum of scooters and jet-skis and music bellowing out of rented convertibles would have made eavesdropping nearly impossible, Gertie instinctively lowered her voice. "The M word has never passed between Gianni and me. Never. And I can't imagine he's involved. Not in a bad way, I mean. Not willingly. He's a kind man, Peter. But things have a way of, you know, getting complicated. All tangled up. Anyway, he asked me to come down here right away and talk to you and see if you would help him."

"Help him? Me? Why me?"

"Why you? Because you're a detective."

"Oh Christ, Mom, you told him that?"

"Of course I did. What, I'm not proud of my son?"

"But I'm not a detective, Mom. Not a real one. You know that as well as I do. The license was just a tax dodge, working the home office angle so I could put a new addition on the house."

"Mr. Modest," said his mother. "Like I don't know all about the cases you solved? Like I didn't keep the clippings from the paper? Like I don't have them Scotch-taped in a little scrapbook?"

"Scrapbook? Mom, listen, I've had my license fifteen years and I've had exactly two clients, and I didn't want either of them."

"Which makes it even more impressive that you solved their cases anyway. Both of them. Two-for-two."

"Mom, let's be real, okay? I didn't solve squat. I didn't unravel any mysteries. I never followed a clue. I never even had a clue to follow. That's not modesty, it's the truth. I hung around till the cases solved themselves. That's all I did. I got lucky."

"So maybe you'll get lucky again. Why not three-for-three? If it's a help to Gianni?"

Pete put down his glass, blew some air out from between puffed cheeks, and glanced with a sort of instantaneous nostalgia around the small backyard that had seemed so peaceful, so safe, so insulated and edenic right up until the moment that his mother had limped in, dragging in her wake this whoosh of tumult from the outside world. "Mom," he said, "listen, I may not be a real detective, but I do know a little bit about what happens when a detective agrees to help someone. It's not like other kinds of helping. It's not like, say, helping someone put groceries in their trunk. That kind of helping has a beginning and an end. There's an exit. Someone says thank you, someone says you're welcome, everybody smiles, and it's over. When a detective says he'll help someone, it never works like that. You don't know where it's going to lead. Or how long it'll take. Or if it'll turn out to be dangerous. And this is whether or not it happens to involve veal chops from New York. You agree to help someone, all you know for sure is that it's going to turn your life upside down, and I don't want my life turned upside down because I like it the way it is."

"You do?" said his mother, with what seemed genuine surprise and even wonderment. "Just sitting around naked on a weekday afternoon? With nobody around? Doing nothing? This is what you like?"

"I wasn't doing nothing, Mom. I was sitting quietly with my mind and senses open wide and I was savoring the moment. That's very different from doing nothing. And it's something they don't teach you up in Jersey. I had to move down here to learn it. And yeah, it what's I like these days. I like it a lot."

Gertie shrugged. "Okay. I guess I understand. Sort of. Not really. People turn out different. So I won't twist your arm. You don't want to get involved with Gianni's troubles, fine. Probably a bad idea to begin with. But would you do me one small favor? Would you at least come with me to see him in the hospital?"

"Hospital? Christ, Mom, this is sounding worse already. Why's he in the hospital? He get his knees broken or hit with a bat or something?"

"God forbid," said Gertie. "No, nothing like that. He fell down playing pickleball. Boom, just like that he went down. That's what he said. Boom, just like that. Tore something in his leg. He's in a cast, I think."

The last of Pete's Champagne had evaporated or maybe boiled away in the mounting humid heat. Wistfully, he sniffed the yeasty vapor at the bottom of the glass then ran a hand over his eyebrows and all the way up to the top of his head. "Mom, listen, I'm sorry he got hurt but I really don't want—"

"To get involved," she put in. "I know. I get it. But this is just a hospital visit. A basic courtesy. Your father and me, we raised you to be courteous, right? Someone moves, you give a house gift. A figurine maybe, a plant. Someone invites you over, you bring cake. Or Danish in a box. Someone's in the hospital, you go to see them. That's just what you do. Basic courtesy."

Pete said nothing. Nothing needed saying. Nothing would have made a difference. He was going to the hospital. That had never really been in doubt. This was his mother, after all.

She started getting up from her chair, trying to hide the effort it cost her, the weight on her wrists pushing up from the table so she could rearrange the balky leg that had gotten stiff from sitting. When she was upright, or nearly so, she said, "Oh, I almost forgot. I still need to bring in my things."

"Your things?"

"Just a couple of small suitcases."

"A couple?"

"I left them on the porch."

"The porch?" echoed Pete, vaguely aware that he was sounding like an idiot but feeling suddenly too dazed to answer otherwise.

"In case you weren't home. I'll bring them in now. Maybe

you could help me. I'll be staying here a while."

"Here?"

"I tried the hotels. All full."

"What about Gianni's place? I thought you'd be staying with Gianni."

"Weren't you listening, Peter? His furniture hasn't arrived yet. I told you that. No bed, no couch, no nothing. So he's staying with a niece of his. Tiny place, he says. And I wouldn't be comfortable staying there with a relative of his I've never even met."

"Suddenly you're a stickler for propriety?"

Gertie let that pass. "I won't be any trouble, Peter. You'll hardly know I'm here. And it'll just be till Gianni's problems get worked out."

"God knows how long that'll take," said Pete.

"Probably less time if he gets some help from a pro," said Gertie, patting her son's hand. "I'll just go freshen up a bit before the hospital.

4.

As hospitals go, Florida Keys Community had pretty good views. Some rooms looked out toward the greens and sand traps of the municipal golf course on Stock Island; some faced the innocent meadow that, before it had been wrapped in plastic and miraculously cooked down, had been the infamous alp Mount Trashmore, Key West's garbage dump full of coffee grounds, fish heads, enough latex condoms to build a blimp, and the decomposing evidence of decades worth of unsolved crimes. Certain privileged hospital rooms even offered glimpses of Gulf-side wetlands filled with pelicans and osprey and egrets.

As for the quality of the medical care, well, Florida Keys Community had pretty good views.

But Gianni Calabro's injury, while serious, was pretty routine and, by the time Gertie and Pete arrived for their visit, his ruptured Achilles had been successfully sutured back together, his left leg armored by a plaster cast wrapped in bright blue stretchy gauze, and he was resting fairly comfortably in an armchair, foot up on an ottoman, fortified by generous doses of pain meds.

At the threshold of his room, Pete hung back a step or two as his mother, with surprising grace, hurtled toward her boyfriend, threw her arms around him as he sat there, and gave him a kiss. It was not a drawn-out, cinematic kiss, but it was on the lips, and this alone was enough to make Pete just slightly dizzy; his aged mother kissing on the lips a man who was not his father—this just wasn't something he'd ever imagined he would see or had even occurred to him as the remotest possibility. It was bizarre. It was uncanny.

The kiss completed, she reached into the huge purse she carried on her shoulder, pulled out a dainty lace-fringed handkerchief, and blotted her smeared lipstick. Then she reached into the purse again and came out with a bag of cookies. "Biscotti," she said. "The kind you like. With pistachios."

Gianni murmured a thank you. The beringed hand went back into the bag and came out with a brick of mortadella. "With green olives," she said. "Your favorite, right?"

"Yeah," he said. "My favorite. Thank you, honey."

Honey? thought Pete.

One more dive into the bag produced a wedge of cheese that could have served as a chock for airplane tires. "Parmigiana," she announced. "Reggiano."

"Sweetheart," Gianni said, "this is very nice of you, but ya think they don't have food down here?"

"Maybe not the things you're used to. Maybe not the quality." She put the bag down and laid a palm across her lover's forehead, exactly as she'd done a thousand times across Pete's when she was checking him for childhood fevers. "So how you feeling, Gianni? Tell the truth, you feel okay?"

"Feelin' good," he said. "Wit' you here, baby, I feel terrific. Ya look so beautiful. Thanks for comin' down so fast."

It was only when these cooing preliminaries had been dispensed with that either Gianni or Gertie seemed to remember that Pete was also in the room. At that point, Gianni finally looked up past his geriatric girlfriend's shoulder and the two men met eye to eye. Though it pained him somehow to acknowledge it, Pete had to admit that Gianni Calabro, though weathered by the years, was still a very handsome man. Still had a full head of thick black hair brushed straight back from his forehead with only a dusting of gray at the temples. Jet-black eyes with plenty of humor in them. Firm jaw, faintly dimpled chin, and just enough lines in his cheeks and at the mouth corners to testify to a fully-lived life. His probing stare melting toward a smile, he said, "Hello, Pete. It's good to see ya. It's been, Jesus Christ, how long? Ya still hate mushrooms?"

"Excuse me?"

"Mushrooms. Still hate 'em? Ya think I don't remember? You and your folks would come in on a Sunday, order an everything pizza wit' extra cheese, and your plate always came back to the kitchen wit' a little pile a picked-off mushrooms on it. I remember stuff about my favorite customers."

Touched in spite of himself, Pete said, "Yeah, I still hate mushrooms. To me they taste like mildewed dirt. Sorry about your Achilles."

The injured man shrugged. "Ah, stuff happens. But I thank you for coming. I'm grateful, I really am. I knew you'd come."

"You did?"

"Your mother, she's always saying what a total mensch you are. Those are her exact words. My son Peter, he's such a total mensch. Always does the right thing. Always."

"Don't believe everything you hear, Gianni. Especially from someone's mother."

"Well, that's another thing she says. How modest you are. Always helping people and never taking credit."

"There's no credit to be taken. But listen, Gianni, I'm glad to see you, but this is just a social call, okay?"

The boyfriend winced slightly as he adjusted his hurt leg on the ottoman. "Social call?" he said. "Okay. So let's be social. Have a seat. Relax. Who wants a biscotto?"

Pete passed but Gertie said she'd love one. Gianni tore open the bag with the big strong hands of a practiced pizzaiolo. She reached in, grabbed a cookie, then retreated to the small room's only vacant chair. Pete leaned back against the hard frame of the bed. There was a moment of awkward silence, then Gianni, to break the ice, said, "So Pete, y'ever play pickleball?"

"Nah, I'm a tennis guy."

"Peter's an excellent tennis player," said his mother.

"No, I'm not."

"He won every single match in high school."

"No, I didn't. I went four-and-six, with two rainouts and one match called because of darkness." To Gianni, he said, "I don't know where she gets this stuff."

The injured man smiled. "Ah, mother love. Just enjoy it while you can, kid. It's a beautiful thing."

Pete didn't quite know what to say to that, so he just crossed his arms and leaned back farther.

After a moment, Gianni went on. "Lotta tennis players, they don't seem to think too much of pickleball. Like it's just a less good game. Whadda you think, Pete?"

What was there to say? Like a lot of the tennis regulars, Pete did in fact secretly suspect that pickleball was a less good game. Then again, he'd never played it. So he just shrugged.

"Some of these guys," said Gianni, "maybe there's a little bit of a turf thing goin' on. Little bit of a snob thing, maybe."

"Maybe," Pete conceded.

"Well, who cares? Main thing is, it's a lotta fun. Less fun if ya end up inna hospital. Well, that's the breaks. But the way this happened…I don't mean the falling down, I mean what led up to the falling down, the why of how it happened, what else was goin' on to make it happen, well, that's what I really wanted to talk to ya about."

Pete raised a palm and said, "Gianni, I'm sorry, but I really don't need or want to hear it. This is just a social call, remember?"

Gianni conveniently didn't seem to hear that. He twitched the lapels of his hospital gown, squared his shoulders, and said, "Gertie, sweetheart, would you mind stepping outside for a couple minutes and leaving the two of us alone?"

She gingerly started rising from her chair. As she rose, Pete's spirits, in perfect but dreadful counterpoint, almost like lukewarm condensation dribbling down while sprightly bubbles floated up, began to sink in anticipation of whatever squalid and distressing and possibly violent details Gianni was so painfully eager to share with him. Absurdly, he had a sudden panicky flashback to that universally terrifying moment on the first day of kindergarten when a little boy realizes he will be left on his own to navigate the outside world with all its riddles and monsters and shadowy places; and right there in Gianni's hospital room, as a grown man in the prime of life, he felt a preposterous impulse to call out, Mom, please don't leave me here. I'm not ready yet. Don't go!

But she did go. She eased herself up from the narrow chair, kissed her boyfriend once again, grabbed another biscotto from the open bag, and sashayed out of the room, her slight limp, perhaps unintentionally, giving her hips a disarmingly coquettish sway.

5.

When the door to the hallway had clicked shut behind her and the two men were alone, Gianni said, "A very fine woman, your mother. Such spirit, so caring. I'm so lucky to have her in my life."

Pete gave a rather non-committal nod.

"You are, too, ya know. Lucky to have her in your life, I mean. How proud she is of you. The way she talks about ya. She musta been an amazing parent when you were growin' up."

"I guess. Didn't have much to compare her to."

"Well, you got a good one, kid. Take my word for it. You got a good one. Devoted. Loyal. Like, fiercely loyal."

There was a pause. Pete looked down at the squares of scuffed gray linoleum on the floor, then started pushing himself up from the edge of the bed. "Well, good, Gianni, thanks for that. And now that we've had our little chat about the virtues of motherhood and how lucky we are, I guess I'll be heading home."

He stood and reached out a hand to shake. Gianni didn't take it. Instead, he looked up at Pete with a brief but unmistakable flash of pleading in his eyes. His voice pinched, he said, "No. Wait. Stay. Please. I really gotta talk to someone."

"Maybe someone else."

"Not someone else. There is no one else. You. Pete, listen, I'm sorry to put this on you, but I'm scared shitless. I really am. Scared shitless and tryin' not to let it show 'cause I don't wanna upset your mother. But someone's after me. I know it. And he wants me to know it. This guy onna pickleball court—"

"Gianni, I'm really not the person for this."

"—he's been followin' me. Stalkin'. And I swear to Christ I don't know why. I don't know what the beef is. And how can you fix a problem if you don't even know what it's about?"

"I have no idea," said Pete. "I only know I want no part of this. Good luck."

Gianni pursed his lips, shifted his leg an inch or two, and turned his weathered face in profile to take a long look out the window at what remained of the old trash dump. In a small voice devoid of accusation but full of disappointment, he said, "Your mother said you'd help me. She was sure you would."

More harshly than he meant to, Pete said, "Well, my mother was wrong."

Without pulling his gaze away from the view, Gianni said, "Okay, my mistake. Shouldn't'a took it at face value. Shoulda known better. Mother love. Sees what it wants to see. Well, no hard feelin's, Pete. I unnerstand."

He folded his hands in his lap. It was a gesture of resignation and the perfect opportunity for Pete to leave. Except he didn't. He just stared down at the linoleum. His mother had boasted to Gianni that her son was a far better person than he knew himself to be. Letting her down would be excruciating, the more so because she'd find a way to keep believing he was wonderful anyway. Then again, living up to her haloed image of him just felt impossible. He was split right down the middle.

He took a long, slow breath, then heard himself say, "Okay, one question, Gianni. This problem you have, um, not to get too personal, not to go anywhere we shouldn't go…it's with the Mob?"

The injured man looked back from the window. He hesitated, then in a raspy voice not much above a whisper, he muttered, "Sure seems that way."

"And you're tied in with them?"

"Don't ask me that. There's this vow guys take. You're not allowed to say."

"Except I think you just did."

Gianni did nothing more than move an eyebrow.

Pete said, "Listen, Gianni, cards on the table, okay? I'm not a tough guy. I haven't punched anyone since junior high, and even then it was only on the arm, and even then I felt shitty about it. I have a gun somewhere but I really don't remember where I put it. And frankly, I'm a coward. If you're in trouble with the Mob, I don't see how—"

"I'm not askin' ya to take a beating for me," Gianni interrupted, "and I'm not askin' ya to be an ass-kicker. Even your mother knows you're not one of those."

"She does? What, she thinks I'm a wuss?"

"She thinks you're too smart to have to fight. She thinks you're a fuckin' genius."

"Shit, that's embarrassing."

"Look, she's your mother. But Pete, all I'm askin' ya to do is listen, see if maybe ya can help me figure out what the hell is goin' on, get it settled wit'out anyone gets killed. Just hear me out, that's all I'm askin'."

Just hear me out, Pete reflected. Wasn't that always how it started? I'm not asking for anything, just listen to my story. People, himself included, didn't seem to realize, until they'd gotten in too deep, that when you listened to a story you became a part of it and the story became a part of you. Even so, he heard himself say, "Okay, Gianni, talk to me."

The hurt man swiveled in his chair and used both hands to rearrange the leg in the heavy cast. "Thank you," he said. "Thank you. So…where the hell to start? Well, okay, I wasn't always inna restaurant business. I was…I did…Let's just say I had a previous profession. I did some other things."

"I kind of thought you might have."

"Nothin' I'm proud of."

"I can imagine."

"Stuff I don't like to talk about."

"Good policy."

"Stuff I wouldn't want your mother to know. It would just upset her."

"Would probably upset me, too," admitted Pete.

"So I'll spare ya the details," said Gianni. "Point is, I did certain things for a while and then there came a time when a powerful man decided for reasons of his own that he didn't want me to keep doin' what I was doin'. He calls me in one day and says, 'Gianni, I'm sorry, but you don't got that job no more. You've become…' What the hell was the word he used? 'You've become a liability. Some high-ups innee other Families, they don't like what you been doin'. They want you gone. So I need you outa the way.'

"So he says this, and I'm shittin' bricks, 'cause when a guy like that says he needs ya outa the way, that usually means outa the way someplace where you're never comin' back. So I say to him, 'Paulie, what the fuck? I been loyal. I been solid, a good earner even when it really wasn't easy. Tough situations, I made the best of 'em, no complaints, even though it grossed me out sometimes. Where'd I go wrong?

"He says to me, 'Ya didn't go wrong, Gianni. Ya did your best. Tough work, what ya did. Took a lotta guts. Lotta guys, most guys maybe, wouldn't'a had the balls to do it. But people see things different, what can I say? Some people didn't like your methods. Bad reflection, some people said. Wrong kind of attention. So you're fired, Gianni. That's just how it is. Accept it and you won't get hurt. You'll still have my protection.'

"So he says this and I'm so relieved I practically start bawlin', but then I think, okay, wait a second, I'm gonna stay alive but my livelihood just went out the window. I got nothin' saved up. I'm fired from the one thing I was good at. What the hell else am I s'posed to do? I got no other skills, no other prospects.

"Well, even while I'm thinkin' this, Paulie, who, don't get me wrong, was basically a brutal prick but also had this kinda surprisin' sentimental side to him, says, 'But listen, Gianni, guys who've done good work for me, I don't leave 'em out inna cold. I find ways to help 'em out. So lemme ask ya somethin'. Y'ever bake a pizza?'

"So," Gianni went on, "long story short, he sends me to work for a nephew of his who runs a red sauce joint out in Jersey City. As an apprentice, like. The deal is that if it turns out I'm a decent cook, and if I can prove I have the savvy to run a place of my own someday, then Paulie'll bankroll me to get started and get me in wit' all the best purveyors."

"Like, for veal chops," Pete put in.

"And steaks. And lobsters. And shrimp. And cheese. So anyway, three, four years I work my ass off. The Jersey City place then a few others, workin' my way up. Dishwasher, pizza man, waiter, line cook, grill guy, manager. One day Paulie calls me in, tells me he hears I'm ready, and hands me the keys to my future. The Grotto in Bloomfield Center. That was thirty-seven years ago. Time flies."

"Good run, thirty-seven years," said Pete, "And this mysterious benefactor, this Paulie, he does this purely out of loyalty? Out of the goodness of his heart?"

Gianni moved his leg an inch too far and winced. "Fuckin' pain pill's wearin' off," he said. Then he added, "Come on, Pete, you're from Jersey. No one does things purely outa loyalty. We had a deal, a split. There were strings attached."

"So lemme guess," said Pete. "The strings got tangled."

"Well, maybe. But here's the thing. I have no idea how or when. I done what I'm supposed to do. Never missed a payment. Never took an extra cent. Hired the guys I was told to hire. I don't know where the fuckup is."

"So why not ask Paulie that?"

"Well, I would, except he died a few months ago."

"Ah, that makes communication difficult."

"And that's when all trouble started. This feelin' that someone's after me. Right after Paulie died."

"So someone took over Paulie's share? I mean, someone's still getting a cut, right?"

"Every fuckin' month."

"So who is it?"

"I don't know."

"You don't know?"

"Look, there's a guy in Paramus. In a strip mall. Mort, his name is. Fat. Bald. Smart. Nice guy. Handles all the money, the tax bullshit, all the back and forth. Says he can't tell me who my new silent partner is. Says that's why they call it silent. So what am I gonna do, argue? He won't tell me, he won't tell me. Prob'ly it's some relative of Paulie's or maybe someone higher up than Paulie who was callin' the shots all along. Whoever he is, he's the guy who basically owns my restaurant."

Pete said, "And for some reason he's pissed off at you."

"Well, that's the crazy part. Supposedly he isn't. Not accordin' to Mort, at least. Accordin' to Mort, everything is copacetic wit' the restaurant."

"Copacetic. So there you go. Problem solved."

"Except it ain't. Or why else would I have some asshole stalkin' me? So maybe it ain't about the restaurant. Maybe it's about the stuff I did a million years ago, this stuff I ain't proud of, that some guys thought got the wrong kind of attention, that still makes me cringe a little if ya wanna know the truth, and that I never told nobody nothin' about—"

"Then maybe it's best you don't start now."

"Except I gotta!" said Gianni, who suddenly looked like he was being strangled by his secrets, his olive skin taking on an unhealthy purplish sheen, blue veins pulsing in his neck. "'Cause now I got this creep shadowin' me, comin' to the restaurant three, four times, followin' me home, somehow trailin' me down here and scopin' out my empty condo where I'm not even livin' yet, then showin' up where I'm playin' pickleball—"

He broke off abruptly because there was a firm knock on the door and then the door swung open although no permission to enter had been granted. Pete's first thought was that his mother, perhaps miffed at being exiled so long to the hallway, had gotten antsy to be let back in, and maybe was being a bit pushy, as she was known to do. But the woman who came sweeping into the hospital room was not Gertie. Rather, she was a vision of fitness and energy and grace in lime-green running shorts and a pale yellow tank-top and shimmering blue sneakers. She had raven hair that framed her jawline and was cut straight across the nape of her neck. Her sunglasses were perched on top of her head, above violet eyes with silver glints. She carried in her wake the smell of sunshine, and before either of the men could speak, she sang out in a bright but low-pitched voice, "Great news, Uncle Gianni. You're kicked out. Discharged. Let's get you up on your crutches. We're going home."

Only after she'd announced her mission did she seem to

notice the man who was leaning back against the edge of the bed. "And you must be Peter."

"Pete."

"I'm Penelope."

She reached out a hand. He took it. She wrapped her other hand around his and looked him in the eye. "I've heard about you, Pete. And I just want to thank you for everything you're doing for Uncle Gianni. It means so much to both of us."

Pete fumbled for a reply. Plus he was in no hurry to end the moment. He liked the feel of his hand being cradled in both of hers. He liked looking at her wide violet eyes, even though he struggled to match the earnestness of her gaze. Finally, he managed, "Well, I haven't done anything yet."

"Yeah, you have," Gianni put in. "You've listened." He reached for his crutches. His niece glided to his side, crouched without effort, and helped ease him up from the chair. "Pete's a great listener," her uncle said to her. "He unnerstands. He gets it."

"Actually, I don't think I do."

"Ah, modest," said Penelope. "Just like your mother says."

"You've met my mother?"

"Just now, out in the hallway. She's very sweet. She's sure things'll work out fine now that you're involved. And you know what, Pete? Even though I've known you for about ten seconds, I sort of feel the same way."

Great, thought the unwilling detective, I inspire blind and total confidence in everyone except myself.

"And I'm wondering," Penelope went on, her firm shoulders unbowed as she supported her slightly wobbly uncle, "if maybe there isn't a little something I could do for you. Something nice. Just to show appreciation."

He looked sideways at her candid violet eyes and swallowed. His legs twitched. He felt a sudden tingling at his hairline. A moment passed.

She said, "You play pickleball, Pete?"

Deflated, befuddled, he said, "Why is everybody asking me that all of a sudden?"

"I teach," explained Penelope. "Was wondering if maybe you'd like some lessons. Private. One-on-one. On the house. Least I could do."

"Um, well, I'm mainly a tennis guy."

"So you'll pick the game up quick. I'll show you a trick or two."

"Well, um…"

"Bet you a dollar you'll enjoy it."

"And maybe," Uncle Gianni put in, "maybe you'd run into the guy that's been hasslin' me. Might be a chance to scope things out."

"Well, um…"

"Open offer," said Penelope. "Call me if you're interested. Your mother has the number."

She flashed a parting smile and led her Uncle Gianni from the room. His blue-wrapped cast looked almost cheerful against the gray linoleum.

6.

In the murky, oystery-smelling shallows just beyond the airport and the seawall, small rays were gliding by in search of crabs and cockles, translucent baby fish were hiding in miniature forests of eel grass, and a stocky man in a torn shirt and ragged cutoff jeans was trying to use a scarred and dented little rowboat as a sailing craft. He had a broomstick for a mast. His sail was a triangle of black webbing fashioned from a windscreen that he'd pilfered from the pickleball courts down at Higgs Beach.

Unfortunately, the scavenged aluminum dinghy was never intended to sail; it had no fitting to accommodate a mast, so the stocky man, whose name was Fred, had no choice but to stand up at the bow and try to hold the broomstick in place, leaning into the breeze at an angle reminiscent of Washington crossing the Delaware. Still, for all Fred's exertions, the hybrid craft made very little progress, and most of its minimal movement was not forward but sideways, so it kept running aground against the coral rocks that dotted the Florida muck. Every time that happened, the would-be skipper had to reach down and grab his one splintered oar so that he could lever the boat off the bottom. Which meant that he had no hands left to hold his fishing pole, even though fishing had been the original aim of the whole misguided expedition.

So, as the sun was getting lower, he eventually dialed back his ambitions. He furled the stolen windscreen, stowed the broomstick, shook out his tired arms, sat down on the sagging thwart, and threw a line in the water.

On land, a mere few hundred yards away, in a secret clearing hidden from both road and sea by an enveloping tangle of waxy mangroves and wispy, gray-green Australian pines, Fred's buddy and roommate, Pineapple, was squatting down to make a campfire of dry twigs and some gnarls of driftwood. He approached the task deliberately, precisely, almost gravely, as he approached everything he did. There was something Old Testament about Pineapple. He was very tall, not skinny, exactly, but somehow stretched, attenuated; he had long unruly hair that hung down to his shoulders, a rather thin and almost negligible beard, and a soft enquiring voice that rarely rose above a murmur. He asked a lot of questions, most of which could not be answered. He seemed to spend a lot of his time just pondering.

He was rethinking and rearranging the geometry of the campfire when Fred came down the narrow path that led into the clearing. "So how was the fishing?" he asked.

"Sucked," said Fred.

Pineapple was accustomed to this outcome, and he softly offered, "Well, we have some other things on hand. Beef stew. Ravioli."

"Fucking boat don't sail worth shit."

"Well, in fairness, Fred, it isn't really a sailboat."

This gave Fred an opening to let out some frustration. He said, "Oh, it isn't, Piney? Then what the hell is it? You have a boat. You have a sail. You put them together. You have a sailboat."

Piney lit the fire, fanned and blew it into life, and thought that over. "Well, I don't know, Fred. Say you have a fire. And say you have a truck. That doesn't give you a fire truck."

"What the hell's that got to do with it?" said Fred, and he stomped off to get himself a beer from the little propane fridge in the abandoned hot dog wagon that the two of them had dragged off from the beach promenade several years before and had called home ever since.

He was still bitching when he came back with his Old

Milwaukee. "Piece a shit can't even get me out to the drop-off. That's where the fish are. At the drop-off. Like, two football fields offshore. That's all it is. Stupid boat can't even get me there."

"Maybe you could row," Pineapple softly suggested. "It is kind of a rowboat, I mean."

This occasioned more venting from Fred. "Oarlocks are busted. Only got one oar. Damn boat's more trouble than it's worth."

Piney kept quiet and tended the fire. It was cooking down nicely, the carefully placed arcs of driftwood gradually collapsing onto the bed of twigs, the flames mellowing down to a pulsing glow. He balanced the cooking grate precisely and said, "Beef stew or ravioli?"

"I don't care," said Fred, who was way more interested in the beer. "You pick."

"Um, I'll take the ravioli. They eat slower."

He opened the cans and put them on the grate. Fred went to fetch another beer. The sun went down. Sunset in the clearing was not the sort of gaudy display that Key West is famous for; it was actually a very muted business. The filmy light that filtered through the pines went from yellow to a brownish red before it was smothered by the opaque mangroves. Shadows faded from glossy black to matte purple then went extinct. Dusk there was less a matter of sight than sound. The crickets and cicadas started up, getting bolder as they went. Tree toads bleated like tiny sheep.

Fred came back and belched. Piney served up dinner. While they were eating, seated on coral rocks on either side of the fire, he said, "Fred, you know what I was just thinking about?"

"No, Piney, I have no idea what you were thinking about."

"I was thinking, well, if the boat isn't doing you any good, and if like you say it's more trouble than it's worth, then I was thinking, well, maybe it would be a good idea to put the windscreen back."

Fred had taken too big a spoonful of stew and it was burning his mouth. He swigged some beer to quell the heat, then said, "Put it back?"

"Well, yeah, put it back. I mean, let's face it, Fred, it really isn't yours, and taking stuff that isn't yours isn't exactly right, let's face it. I mean maybe, okay, if the thing you take isn't doing the other person any good but it would really be a help to you, well, okay, maybe that's an excuse to take it, even though that still doesn't make it right, let's face it. But if maybe it was useful to the other guy and it's doing you no good anyway, what's the excuse for holding on to it? So I was thinking maybe you should put it back."

Fred spooned up more stew. "Forget about it, Piney. I can't put it back."

"How come?"

"How come?" He put his spoon down and clenched his jaw. "How many reasons you want? First of all, I can't put it back 'cause I cut the clamps that were holding it up. So the clamps are shot. Second of all, I can't put it back because, even if I had the clamps, putting it up would take way more time than tearing it down, which means there's way more chance I'd get caught, and how stupid would it be to get in trouble while I'm returning something that I totally got away with grabbing? And third of all, since you insist on making this some highfalutin' bullshit about right and wrong and other happy horseshit you hassle me with from time to time, I'm not gonna put it back because it wasn't doing anybody any good anyway."

Piney was contemplating a raviolo as he listened. He held it on the tip of his fork and just looked at it a while, at the nub of meat and painterly smear of tomato sauce that clung to it. Then he said, "How you know that, Fred? That it wasn't doing anybody any good, I mean?"

"How do I know it? I'll tell you how I know it. I know it because when I went onto the court to grab the screen, it wasn't even windy in there."

"Well, maybe that's because there was a windscreen up before you took it down."

Fred chugged the rest of his beer and crushed the can in his fist. "Goddammit, Piney, will you please just let it go? I'm not putting the fucking windscreen back, and that's the end of it."

The tall man kept quiet, looked down at the fire, and went back to eating ravioli. He ate them one at a time, gently nibbling at the crinkly edge before biting in. He could never understand why some people, Fred for instance, shoveled two or three into his mouth at once. You lost the whole shape of them that way. While he was pondering this, Fred went off to get another beer.

When the stocky man came back to his rock, Piney said casually, "So, yesterday, when I was walking down the beach, I saw something kind of interesting. Kind of a coincidence, I guess you'd say."

"Oh yeah? Wha'd ya see?"

"Well, I was walking all the way down the promenade, past the showers, past the food trucks, past the big bend in the road, all the way to Higgs—"

"I get the picture, Piney. What the hell'd ya see?"

"Well, I saw an ambulance."

"Ah. Somebody drown? Get run over by a jet-ski?"

"Nah, the ambulance guys were working on the land side of the road. On the pickleball courts. And here's the part that's kind of weird. Most of the pickleball courts I couldn't see into. Why? Because they had their windscreens up. So the only court I could see into was the one without the windscreen, and that's where this guy was lying, kind of rolling on his back like a flipped-over cockroach while the ambulance guys were getting the stretcher ready. And I was just thinking how strange it was that all these things should go together.

That that's the court where the windscreen was missing. That that's where the guy gets hurt. That it's the only court I can see into, even just to know it happened. I mean, if you think about it, every little piece of that could've worked out different. Why did it happen that all those different pieces fell together? I mean, if you think about it, lots of things are strange, but this was really strange."

Fred looked down at the fire then said from underneath his eyebrows, "So now it's my fault that some jerk gets hurt?"

"I never said that, Fred. You feeling guilty or something? I'm just saying it's kind of interesting the way things hang together. I mean, like, does one thing cause the next thing to happen? Or do things just happen in a certain order because that's just the way they happen, and then it only seems like one thing led to another, but maybe the second thing was gonna happen even if the first thing didn't."

"Well, it wasn't my fault," said Fred. "Guy falls down, he falls down. Ambulance shows up, it shows up. Say la vee, my friend."

Pineapple finally finished up his dinner, fished a bandanna from a back pocket, and daintily wiped his lips. He picked up an unburnt stick and made a few adjustments to the dimming fire, keeping it symmetrical. Then he said, "Fred, you gonna use that boat anymore? The sailing part, I mean?"

"Hell no. Like I said, too goddamn much trouble. Way more trouble than it's worth."

"Then would you mind if I gave the windscreen back?"

"Piney, Christ, I already told you—"

"I know, I know. About the clamps. I'm not gonna try to hang it up. I'll just leave it there sometime. Maybe someone else can put it back. I'd just like to get it off my conscience."

"Your conscience? What the hell's it got do with your conscience. I'm the one who grabbed the thing."

"Yeah, but I'm the one who saw the ambulance. So I'd just feel better bringing it back."

Fred shrugged. "Okay, Piney, I happen to think it's a piss-poor idea, but okay, go ahead, do whatever the hell ya want. But I'll give ya one piece of advice, my friend. Don't get caught while you're tryin' to clear your conscience. It'll only lead to trouble."

7.

"Nice, isn't she?" said Gertie, as Pete was driving them home from the hospital.

It was twilight, that time when dusk on U.S. 1 gets all jangled up with pulsing neon signs and glaring headlights and the final flashes of reflected sun through broken slabs of cloud. They'd just crossed over the Cow Key Bridge and were heading down the Boulevard past the ever-spreading clusters of stilted townhomes in gumdrop colors of pink and green and blue. Very cheery, those little houses, very tropical. The only problem was that the more they tried to look like old Key West, the less like Key West they felt. Key West was never meant to be that tidy. Key West wasn't so obsessively planned, so relentlessly pastel. Key West just happened, just sort of fizzed up, moment by moment. These new places had the look of stage sets for scripted comedy or melodrama; but the real Key West had more the feel of a rollicking and messy audience-participation improv show haphazardly performed on street corners or sagging porches.

"Hmm?" Pete said. He hadn't been listening to his mother or focused on the scenery. He'd been thinking about the mix of playfulness and earnestness and teasing in Penelope's violet eyes. He'd been wondering if maybe she'd hold his arm and lean her body against his while teaching him proper pickleball technique.

"Gianni's niece. She seems like a very nice girl."

"Yeah, I guess."

"We had a nice chat in the hallway."

"That's nice."

"You know what she told me? She told me she moved down here about a year and a half ago, and she's been on her own the whole time. I found that surprising. An attractive girl like that. Why would she be on her own? Maybe she had some terrible experience."

"Or maybe she didn't," said Pete, following his usual impulse to sidestep unpleasantness. "Why go to the dark side, Mom? Maybe it's just that she has standards."

"What, and I don't?" said Gertie.

"Mom, who said anything about you? We weren't talking about you. We're talking about Penelope. You said you're surprised she's on her own. I said maybe she has standards, and standards tend to sludge up the romantic process. This has nothing to do with you."

"Well, it so happens I have standards, too. High standards, thank you very much."

"I never said you didn't."

"But I just don't see why people would rather be alone."

"How about because it's simpler, Mom. Quieter. You don't have someone jumping down your throat for making an innocent remark."

"I wasn't jumping down your throat. But it hurt my feelings a little bit, that crack about my standards."

"Mom, it wasn't about—"

"Okay, okay, you didn't mean it. I accept your apology. Let's move on."

They were cruising past Garrison Bight Marina by then. Listing houseboats with flaking paint jobs squeaked and groaned against their pilings. Shirtless locals with rosewood suntans and prodigious beer-bellies pedaled by on fat-tire bikes with chopper handlebars. The town felt like itself again.

As they hung a right onto Eisenhower, Gertie changed the subject. "So, your talk with Gianni. It went well?"

"About as well as it could go between a guy who can't decide how much he wants to say and a guy who really doesn't want to hear it anyway."

"So wha'd he tell you?"

"Mom, if he wanted you to know, he wouldn't have asked you to leave the room."

"You're not being very communicative, Peter. Or pleasant. First you say I have no standards, then I ask you a simple question and you get all snippy."

He turned left onto Petronia and started easing toward the cracked curb where the roots of the traveler palm had lifted the sidewalk in front of his house. As he parked, he said, "Okay, Mom, you want communication? Let's communicate. Let me ask you a question. Why is it that when you talk to other people, you praise me to the skies, like, way beyond what I or anybody else deserves or could possibly live up to, but when it's just the two of us, you sort of have a lifelong tendency to bust my chops? Why is that, Mom?"

"I bust your chops?" she said, with an innocent and slightly puzzled look. That was as much of an answer as she offered.

They went into the house. He pulled out fresh towels and got her settled in the guest bedroom next to the sound-proof chamber where he stored his wine and listened to music. Then he told her he had an appointment downtown and needed to go out a while.

This was a fib. He didn't have an appointment. He wanted a quiet drink. The crazy part was that, right there in his own home, he had a padded room stocked with all his favorite wines—Sancerre, Trousseau, Poulsard—and yet a quiet drink seemed impossible with his mother in the house. True, the triple-insulated door would block all sound; unfortunately, though, sound was not the only kind of noise. There was also the emotional noise that you sensed through

43

your pores rather than your ears. There was the noise of conscience that clamored in the pit of your stomach. There was the noise of preoccupation with its relentless grating just beneath the scalp.

Those silent kinds of noise were harder to block out, and so, perversely, there were times in life when a person's best chance at a quiet drink was in a noisy public place where the noise, at least, had nothing to do with him.

8.

So he fetched out his old blue bike from the narrow, weedy side yard and pedaled down to the Eclipse Saloon.

The Eclipse was near, but not on, Duval Street, and this was crucial. If the place had fronted on the famous strip and paid rent accordingly, it would have needed to offer dubious attractions such as wet t-shirt contests, cocktails made with Jell-o, and live music featuring mediocre covers of songs that everyone had already heard way too many times in way too many places. As it was, the Eclipse offered draught beer, honest drinks with honest pours, and a fish sandwich in which the grouper filet stretched out beyond the confines of the roll, and extra napkins were provided on the assumption that customers would use their fingers to pick up the pieces that fell off. There was a U-shaped bar with worn leather padding where long-haul drinkers could rest their elbows. The dark-paneled walls were festooned with trophy fish left over from the bad old days when sport fishermen would keep their catch. Tourists were welcome as long as they didn't act too much like tourists.

When Pete came through the doorway, the place was mostly empty and Nell was tending the bar, dressed for work as always in cutoffs, a men's shirt with the tails tied across her midriff, and a bandanna, Rosie-the-Riveter style, knotted just above her forehead. She lifted an eyebrow in his direction when he was still three strides away. He responded with a thumbs-up. That's all it took for her to reach down to the fridge and pour him a big glass of the least bad white wine they had. She was serving it to him before he was even settled on his stool. This was the beauty of a neighborhood joint.

"Cheers," he said, as he raised it to his lips.

"Cheers, Pete. Everything okay with you? Haven't seen you in a while."

"Been laying low," he said. "Just treating myself to some quiet time at home. Super low-key. Been very nice. That ended today. My mother came to town."

Not knowing Pete's mother, Nell said, "That must be nice for you."

"Yes and no. How're things with you?"

"All good. Work's been mostly mellow. Been getting to the beach, playing pickleball."

"Pickleball? You too? What's up with that? It's all I've been hearing lately. Pickleball this, pickleball that. Can't get away from it all of a sudden."

"You should try it, Pete. It's fun."

Skeptically, he said, "That's what people keep telling me. I even got offered free lessons today. By a gorgeous woman, no less."

"Penelope?"

"You know Penelope?"

"Not really. I've seen her giving lessons down at Higgs. Terrific player. Amazing mover."

"I can only imagine."

They shared something that wasn't quite a wink, then Nell slid off to draw a Guinness for another customer.

When she came back, Pete murmured, "Pickleball. What a dumb name. But all of a sudden it's everywhere. It's even the reason, sort of, that my mother came to town."

"Your mother plays?"

"Nah. It's a little complicated. My mother's boyfriend…except I didn't know until today she had a boyfriend…he plays, and, well, it turns out he's the guy who ran this pizza joint that we went to all the time when I was a kid…except, as it turns out, it wasn't just a pizza joint but also did veal chops and some other fancy things that, up in Jersey, well, let's just say have connotations. But anyway, no, my mother doesn't play. She's has a fake hip and limps a little."

"Doesn't stop a lot of other people," Nell put in. "You should see the scars, the braces. There's enough Ace bandage on those courts to lasso Cuba."

He raised his glass. "Well, a toast to the wounded warriors. But anyway, my mother doesn't play, but she has this boyfriend…" Then he suddenly stopped himself. "Nell, I'm sorry. You must have to listen to other people's shit day in, day out."

"You kidding? Best part of the job. Go on."

"Really? Well, okay. So she has this boyfriend who I didn't even know about until, like three hours ago, and it turns out he plays pickleball down here, and yesterday he took a fall—"

"Wait a second," said Nell. "Was it on court six?"

"I don't know what court. A court's a court, right?"

"Except six is the one without a windscreen. And if this is the guy who went down on court six, I was his partner when it happened."

"So you know him?"

"Nah, never met him before. It was a pick-up game, we just got put together. Johnny, right?"

"Gianni," Pete corrected.

"Whatever. Seemed like a nice guy."

Pete took a swig of wine, gave his face and eyes a rub, shook his head, and slowly exhaled. "Jesus, talk about a small world. This guy shows up out of nowhere, and it just happens to turn out he's your partner, my mother's boyfriend, Penelope's uncle, and my headache."

"Penelope's uncle?"

"Yeah. He's staying at her place. Which is why my mother's staying at mine. I told you it was complicated."

"And why your headache?"

"Why my headache? Look, Nell, it's best I don't go into it too far, but Gianni, aside from having a torn Achilles, seems to have certain Jersey-style problems that my mother, God knows why, seems to think that only I can solve, except I can't. And then Penelope comes into it and also forms this crazy notion that I'm the guy who can make her uncle's problems go away, and so she greets me very warmly and holds my hand and stares into my eyes and offers to teach me some tricks—pickleball tricks, you understand—as a thank you in advance. Except the simple truth is I just don't want to get involved."

"With Penelope?"

"With Gianni. Penelope's an open question."

"Probably be more open if you help her uncle."

A couple of tourists straggled in and sat at the far end of the bar. Nell moved across to take their order. They asked for margarita slushies. She told them she didn't have a slush machine. They left.

In the brief interval when he was sitting there alone, his wineglass mostly empty now, Pete, in spite of himself, was taking baby-steps toward where he didn't want to go. When Nell came back, he said, "So, the fall. You saw it happen?"

"Well yeah, sure, in a sideways kind of way. He was chasing a shot. The ball got caught up in the wind. He sort of lunged at it, then

48

he crumpled."

"Any chance he got distracted by someone he didn't want to see?"

"I couldn't tell. I mean, I was wrapped up in the game. But that's what Bert thought. Old Bert. You know him, right?"

"Bert the Shirt?" said Pete. "Of course I know him. Everybody knows him. He's helped me out a couple times. But, for fuck's sake, don't tell me he plays pickleball, too. I mean, who else? Mahatma Gandhi? Julius Caesar? Napoleon?"

"He doesn't play. Just watches from the bleachers. Part of his routine, I guess, when he's out with the dog. Anyway, he was watching from a few courts away, so he had a different angle. You're interested, maybe you should talk to him. Another drink?"

Pete pursed his lips and peered down to gauge the level of his wine. He judged it to be about a pinky's width, and this was an inflection point where a drinker had basically three choices: Slam it down and start wading through a fresh one; or keep nursing it even though it had gotten warm and flabby; or let it sit and go home for something better. "Think I won't," Pete said, "but can I get a couple of fish sandwiches to go? One with mushrooms, one without. Gonna be a good boy and bring dinner home for Mom."

9.

"No vegetables?" said Gertie.

"Mom, it's from a bar. Bars just aren't that big on vegetables. There's lettuce and tomato on the roll."

They were sitting at the little table by the pool, whose submerged blue light cast a serene glow upward at the misted stars. The baked smells of afternoon had shed their astringent tang and been replaced by the faintly artichoke perfume of the day's exhausted flowers. Pete had taken the sandwiches out of their cardboard containers and put them onto proper dinner plates. They'd fallen apart during the transfer, flakes of fish and curls of sautéed onion tumbling into mystic patterns around the edges of the now floppy and lopsided rolls; he tried his best to put them back together without his mother noticing, then opened a bottle of vinho verde, which with its slight fizz and sizzle of acidity was about as close as one could come to a good match for a soggy grouper sandwich.

With a deftness that was surprising, given her swollen knuckles and phalanx of heavy rings, Gertie lifted the fragile assemblage to her lips and took a righteous bite. "Better than it looks," she said.

"High praise. I'll tell the chef."

A few bites later she put the sandwich down and said, "Peter, I was thinking about what you said to me before."

"Hmm?"

"That I pick on you. Or bust your chops, I think was what you said."

"Ah, don't worry about it, Mom. It was a stressful moment. It's been a stressful day."

"But you said I always do it. Do I? Do you think I always bust your chops?"

He sipped some wine and thought it over. Then he said, "Always? No. Sometimes. Fairly often. And let's face it, sometimes I deserve it. I can be a real jerk sometimes."

She reached across the table to pat his hand and tilted her head at a sympathetic angle. Her son waited for her to reassure him that, no, he wasn't a real jerk sometimes. Instead, she said, "Well, everyone's a jerk sometimes."

"Oh thanks, I feel much better now."

"Peter, I didn't mean—"

"Yeah, I know, I know. I guess it's just that, for some odd reason, I seem to feel like more of a jerk more of the time when you're around to point it out."

"Well, I never mean to do that, honey. I adore you, Peter. You know I do."

He fiddled with his napkin. "Well, yeah, I know it. Sort of. But you know what it is, Mom? It's like, when you're around, I have three different guys wrestling inside my skin. There's the guy you think I am. There's the guy I think I am. And then there's the guy I really am. It just gets a little crowded in there sometimes."

Gertie picked up the rest of her sandwich. Before having any, she said, "No one expects you to be perfect, Peter. Not even me, and I'm your mother."

He drained his wine, wiped his lips, pushed his plate away, and said, "Thanks for that, Mom. Love you, too. But now I need to go out again."

"Go out? Again you're going out? This afternoon all you did

was sit there naked doing nothing and said that's how you like it, and now all you do is run around."

"Things change fast sometimes," he said. "There's an errand I need to run before it gets too late. It's about Gianni. I'm trying to be helpful, Mom. I really am."

10.

When Pete's call came in about getting together to discuss the pickleball mishap, Bert the Shirt was just getting ready to take Nacho out for his nighttime walk.

This was a more complicated process than might offhand be imagined. First, the old man had to stick his head out the living room window of his apartment at the Paradiso Condominium to determine if he and the dog would need to put on one of their several matching cardigans sets; it was January, after all, and even in Key West, especially right across the street from the Atlantic Ocean, the evenings tended to be sweater weather, more so given the limited insulation in a lean old man and a four pound chihuahua with hardly any hair.

Feeling a slight chill, Bert decided that the light alpaca ensemble in burnt sienna would probably be best, but then he had to remember what drawer he'd stashed the garments in. Once he'd found them, he had to wrestle Nacho, paw by paw, into the tiny sweater, but the dog, excited to the point of frenzy about the prospect of a walk, kept spinning around and thrashing its tail and poking its legs through the wrong holes and getting tangled up and falling on the floor. Eventually the dog was dressed, but then Bert still had to dress himself, and this too required some time and care, because Bert was not the sort of man who would go out in public without his shirt collar and placket lying just so and the shoulders of his cardigan draping smoothly and symmetrically, a la Perry Como. When he was finally satisfied at the mirror, he had to go searching for his house keys, which he'd told himself a thousand times to always drop in the same place so it would be easier to find them, but then he would forget to do that. The keys located, he'd often be halfway out the door when he remembered to go back for a dog-doo bag. Then he'd sometimes forget why he'd gone in, and would have to go out again to think back and reconstruct the process. Then he'd sometimes make an extra trip inside for a second dog-doo bag, just in case Nacho was indecisive or feeling spiteful that evening and wound up spreading the wealth and making Bert do two swoops downward to pick up shit.

By the time he'd made it down the elevator to the lobby, Pete had biked crosstown and been waiting for him twenty minutes.

"Sorry to hold y'up," the old man said. "Damn dog. It's like dressin' Lady Gaga. Anyway, y'in a hurry?"

Pete said that he wasn't.

"Come on then, let's walk. I'll show y'exactly where it happened."

So they picked their way across A1A, dodging rented scooters and convertibles with their radios blasting, and headed down the promenade that flanked Smathers Beach, past the restrooms and the showers, through the driveway of the fancy condo plastered all over with Private Property No Trespassing signs that everybody used as a shortcut anyway. Here and there, Nacho stopped to sniff and pee. A crescent moon was close to setting, sending a reflection across the waveless water in the exact shape of a banana. As they neared the cluster of bocce courts at White Street, the crisp dry click of colliding balls could be heard above the crickets and the cooing doves. Finally, in a patch of scrub, Nacho leaned back on his haunches and looked at Bert with that curiously pleading stare that all dogs, who knows why, seem to fix on their masters when they're shitting. The old man held the little creature's gaze for as long as was required, then said to Pete, "I hope to Christ it's one-and-done. The bending over's killing me."

He fished in his pockets for the doo-bag. For a fleeting instant, Pete considered volunteering to take over the unpleasant chore, but didn't. It was not his dog and he had his limits, though lately it seemed like they were being tested hourly.

They strolled on toward Higgs Beach, the straight sidewalk now becoming a winding path strewn with errant sand that crunched beneath their feet. Across the roadway, on the stanchions above the pickleball courts, the timered lights suddenly switched off, but rather than going dark all at once, they did a slow fade from bright white to butter yellow to acid orange to the sad red of a dying star. A few diehards kept right on playing as night engulfed the courts. The pickleballs spun and faintly glowed like satellites in low orbits. From outside the fence, Bert pointed out the fateful court six.

"That's the one," he said. "Wit'out the windscreen. He was onna side a the court closer to the ocean and he went down like a tonna bricks. But come on, I'll show ya my exact whaddyacallit, vantage point or my perspective so to speak, and I can give ya the play-by-play or blow-by-blow a what I saw and my personal impression or ya could say interpretation a the unfortunate event."

So they climbed into the bleachers in the dimness, the dog's toenails ticking and slipping over the aluminum seats until Bert picked him up and carried him. A few people were packing up their gym bags. A few were sucking beers and chatting. At the far end, there was reefer being smoked, and underneath the structure a couple of guys were sleeping on flattened cardboard boxes.

"So what happened," Bert said, after they had settled in, "the way it looked to me at least, is he's chasin' the ball, he's watchin' it like you're s'posed to, then he looks up, then he looks down at the ball again, then he looks up again, but the second time he looks up, he's got this oh shit expression on his face. It's hard ta describe. His mouth is open. His eyebrows go up. Anyway, it's that oh shit expression. Everybody knows it when they see it, right? He's got that on his kisser, he yells somethin' out, then he goes down."

"What'd he yell?" asked Pete.

"Well, there's a bone a contention about that. One side says he yelled out son of a bitch. The other side says they heard you son of a bitch, which I would imagine or even presume woulda been directed toward the guy onna next court who he was lookin' at when he got the oh shit expression."

"So which was it? What did he yell?"

"Pete, I was sittin' far away and I'm an old man wit' hair in my ears. I really couldn't tell ya."

"So who's the guy he was yelling at?"

"An excellent question," said the old man. Then he shrugged. "I have no idea. I mean, before all this happened, I hardly noticed the guy. Why would I? Prob'ly a tourist, why waste time? Then, after the poor guy took the header, everybody was watchin' him rollin' around onna ground, and by the time I thought to look back at the guy who maybe caused or let's just say was at least a possible factor innee incident, the people from the other court were leavin', and all I think I remember was that he was a big guy and he had black hair."

"Well, that narrows it down," said Pete.

Bert rubbed the dog's head like he was rubbing his own chin. "Actually," he said, "it does. I mean, I wouldn't'a noticed he had black hair if he had a hat on, and almost everybody else was wearin' hats inna broilin' sun. So I think we can conclude or at the very least hypotenuse, or hypothesize I guess the word would be, that he's a big guy wit' black hair who don't like hats. Better'n nothin'."

Pete nodded, silently admitting that Bert, if he hadn't been a criminal for the first half century or so of his career, would have made an excellent detective. About a thousand times better than himself.

"An' this now brings it up to my turn t'ask a couple questions," the old man went on, "and I will preface this, or lead into it if you prefer, by acknowledgin' that more than once in my life people have accused me a bein' a little, let's say overly curious about other people's business, or even just plain nosy, to call it what it is, and this is a charge I cannot deny but I ain't ashamed of either, 'cause if people weren't curious about what other people were up to or you might say goin' through, then the world would be a pretty cold and borin' place. At least that's my opinion. So I'll take nosy every time. Which brings me to my question. This guy who took the header, what the hell's it got to do wit' you?"

Pete braced himself and said, "Well, he's my mother's boyfriend."

"You have a mother? I mean, wait, that's not what I mean. Everybody has or, in many cases as we ourselves grow ancient and slouch toward our inevitable demise, which is no big tragedy but simply how it is 'causa Adam and Eve and that bullshit wit' the apple, used to have a mother. But what I'm askin' is does your mother live down here?"

"No, thank God."

"That was pretty whaddyacallit, emphatic," Bert observed.

"Guess it was a shitty thing to say. Just slipped out. But no, she doesn't live down here. She lives in Jersey. So does the boyfriend. But he wants to be a snowbird. Just bought a condo but it isn't furnished yet so he's staying with his niece."

"Wait a sec," said Bert. "He the guy who just bought 3F at the Paradiso?"

"I don't know where he bought. So you've met him?"

"Nah, this is just gossip inna building. That a guy from up north bought 3F but his furniture is stuck in Singapore or some other town in China. Might be the same guy, who knows?"

"Just my luck," said Pete, unhappily reflecting that Gianni might now turn out to be not only his mother's boyfriend, Penelope's uncle, Nell's partner, and his headache, but Bert's future neighbor as well. Why did everything have to be so tangled up and braided in this dinky island town? "Anyway, the guy has a problem. He thinks someone has a grudge against him—"

"The big guy onna next court?" Bert put in.

"Maybe. He doesn't know. That's the weird part. He doesn't seem to have any idea who's mad at him or why. So he asked me to help him figure it out, which I really didn't want to do, but my mother's leaning on me to do it, and his niece, who happens to be drop-dead gorgeous, is hoping I'll do it, so I said I'd try."

"Nice a ya."

"Be nicer if I could do it without the lousy grudging attitude, but anyway, I'm doing it. So I wondered if maybe I should talk to you...if maybe it might be helpful...if you might have some particular insight because, I mean, well, you know——"

"So it's Mafia? Come on, Pete, spit it out. It's not like it's a deep dark secret anymore. I mean, it's been playin' on reruns twenty years, how secret can it be?"

"Well, okay, thanks. Yeah, it's Mafia. The boyfriend, I think he was probably a pretty low-level New York wiseguy thirty-five, maybe forty years ago."

"What kinda wiseguy? Collector? Enforcer? Driver? Numbers guy? Private lender? Protection department? Sanitation? Roads and bridges? Union work? I mean, we were a pretty perversified operation back then."

"No idea," said Pete. "He said he'd spare me the details."

"Very commendable," said Bert. "We coulda used a few more guys who knew when ta keep their fuckin' mouth shut. So what's his name, this guy."

"Calabro. Gianni Calabro. Guess he'd be around sixty, sixty-five by now. Been running a restaurant in Jersey for thirty-something years."

"Calabro, Calabro," mulled Bert, and eased into a long slow spasm of scratching Nacho between the ears. The dog twisted its head this way and that in its masters crotch, not wanting to leave a millimeter unpetted. Finally the old man said, "Sorry, Pete, I seem to be drawin' a blank...unless, hang on a sec...nah, it couldn't be...well unless...shit, it's all I'm comin' up wit'...unless it was a guy named

Gianni the Horse Calabro."

"The Horse?" said Pete.

"Yeah, the Horse," Bert confirmed. "Nickname he picked up. Ya know. On accounta…well, on accounta some of the stuff he did, kinda got known for."

Feeling suddenly queasy, Pete said, "Like, um, what kind of stuff?"

"Well, if it's the guy I'm thinkin' of, and who knows, maybe it is, maybe it isn't, and maybe ya wanna hear this and maybe ya don't, given that I gather he's on let's say intimate terms wit' your mother, but y'asked the question, and when y'ask a question ya gotta be ready for an answer, so, well, the answer is that if this Gianni is the Gianni I'm thinkin' of, i.e. Gianni the Horse, well, he used to run a strip club."

"Strip club," echoed Pete, briefly picturing the standard images of women shaking their pasties or sliding down greased poles, then trying to decide where strip club management would fall on the broad and subtle spectrum of moral offenses that Gianni might have been involved with.

He was still wrestling with the question when Bert went on. "And this strip club had, like, a twist to it. A novelty, ya might say."

"Novelty?"

"Yeah, a novelty. Ya know, a gimmick."

Against his better judgment, Pete said, "And the gimmick was…?"

Bert cleared his throat and glanced out toward the ocean. "Well, the gimmick was that the stripper was him."

"Him?"

"Yeah, him. Gianni the Horse. One night a week. Ladies

Night. He'd kinda switch things around, let the ladies be the ones to watch. Why not? On'y fair. Me, I never caught his act but I heard that he was very entertainin'."

"I think I'm gonna puke."

"What, Pete? All of a sudden you're a prude?"

"I'm not a prude, but for Chrissakes, Bert, this is my mother we're talking about. She's close to eighty. She limps. It's just a little difficult to get my mind around the idea that she's having a fling with a stripper called the Horse."

"Yeah," the old man conceded, "I could see where that might be a little tough. So ya know what, just fuhgeddabout it. Don't picture it or anything. Just put it outa your mind."

"Yeah, right."

"Besides, maybe we're not even talkin' about the same guy heah. Maybe I got the name screwed up. Wouldn't be the first time. Besides, your guy, didn't ya say he was more of a muscle guy, an enforcer type?"

"Well, yeah, that's what I thought. I mean it's sort of the default, right? Arm-twister. Knee-breaker. But now that I think about it…"

He leaned back against the aluminum bleachers that had turned cold against his shoulder blades and tried his damnedest to remember exactly what Gianni had told him at the hospital. Truth was, he could not recall a single word about fighting or intimidation or any references at all to violence. All Gianni had said was that he'd done some things he wasn't proud of. Things he didn't want Gertie to know about because they would upset her. Things his boss had commended him for, then told him to stop doing.

"Shit, Bert," he went on, "now that I think about it, I really don't know squat about what my mother's Gianni did or didn't do."

Nacho had started rooting around in the fragrant folds and

hollows of his master's pants, so Bert rubbed his ears to quiet him down. Then he said, "Well, it ain't really any a my business 'cept as a friend who's been consulted and confided in, but just as one possible strategy or stratagem, which I'm never sure if they mean the exact same thing but which I believe to be a time-tested tactic and generally a fruitful one, is that if ya don't know squat about what Gianni did or didn't do, maybe ya should ask him."

"But then I'd know."

"Yeah, that is often the outcome of askin' a question."

"But what if I don't want to know?"

"Ah. That's a complication. But I guess I unnerstand, it bein' your mother wit' a limp and all. But onnee other hand, and correct me if I'm wrong, I believe you said a couple minutes ago that this guy Gianni, be he stripper Gianni or ass-kicker Gianni or some other Gianni altogether, has a problem that might be a vendetta 'cept he don't know where the fuck it's comin' from. Is this correct so far?"

Pete admitted that it was.

"And you also indicated and in fact said in plain and simple English that you would like to help this guy, even though you're goin' about it wit' a kinda stinkin' attitude which, no offense, I didn't say that, you did. So my question is, if a guy has a problem that he don't know where it's comin' from, and if you'd like to help him solve this problem, how the fuck are you gonna help if you don't know what the problem is 'cause you're too fuckin' delicate or sensitive or too much of a prude to face up to what he did or didn't do?"

"Bert, it's my mother."

"Which I believe has been established."

"But with a stripper?"

"Stripper, shmipper. Look, your mother seems to care about the guy. To be happy with 'im. To be findin' some joy at a stage a life where joy is not the easiest thing to come by, trust me. And which has absolutely zilch to do wit' how he made his livin' forty years ago and if it happened to involve a little prancin' around in a jockstrap. So ya want my advice?"

"Do I have a choice?"

"My advice is that, inna famous words of Abraham Lincoln unless maybe it was George Washington or from a movie I saw sometime, who knows, is that the truth is your friend, even when it sure as shit don't look that way, and now that I think of it, it mighta been what's-his-name, Clint Eastbrook, but where I'm goin' wit' this is that if you're tryin' to get somewhere, pretty much anywhere, the shortest route is by way of the truth, which, by the way, prob'ly also has the least traffic whereas Bullshit Boulevard is always jammed. So my advice, which you are totally welcome not to follow and I would never be offended if ya didn't, is that if ya wanna help this Gianni guy and also maybe do a solid for your mother, you should get the hell over yourself and have a talk wit' him."

11.

Not long after Pete and Bert and Nacho left the bleachers, Pineapple came walking down the winding path that flanked Higgs Beach. He was wearing Goodwill bathing shorts in a color that had once been olive green and a faded workshirt that had lost its sleeves, and he walked not in the center of the path but at the very edge, avoiding the narrow cones of light that spilled down from the ornamental streetlamps. The sole of one of his sandals had come unglued and it flapped as he walked. Under one arm he carried a heavy and unwieldy roll of thick black fabric; he had to lean like a windblown palm to keep it balanced between the crook of his elbow and his hip.

When he reached the end of the path, he hesitated. He was then directly across the road from the entrance to the pickleball courts; the road was brightly lit and therefore dangerous. A cop car could come cruising by at any moment. A county guard could appear out of nowhere on a golf cart. Pineapple lingered in the shadows until he judged his chances to be about as good as they were likely to get, and then he ran across the roadway as fast as his flapping sandal would allow. The roll of fabric bent double from the bouncing and he half-dragged it behind him as he stumbled along.

He was panting by the time he reached the far side of the street. But the courts themselves, beyond the chain-link fence with its nearly complete array of opaque windscreens, were comfortingly dark, and he grew relatively relaxed as he hugged the fence-line and closed in on the completion of his errand.

So he was utterly unprepared for the blinding flash of cold white light that hit him in the face as he was crossing court three. By reflex, he raised his hands to shield his eyes. The unfurling windscreen fell at his feet.

A voice said, "Fuck you doin' in here, dirtbag?"

Panicked, sightless, the ragged man said softly, "Wasn't doin' nothin'."

For an instant the harsh light shone down on the windscreen. "You plannin' on sleepin' here, dirtbag?"

It was a not unreasonable guess. All over Key West, homeless people were sleeping on or under tarps that looked a lot like that. But the ragged man said, "No, I ain't. I got a place to stay."

The light came up and stung his eyes again and the voice sneered. "And ain't you proud of that?"

"Well, yeah, sorta. I am."

"Good for you, dirtbag. And now you need to get the fuck outa here. This here's a private court."

The concept didn't quite register with Pineapple. "Um, I thought it was a park."

"Are you stupid or what? For right now it's a private court. I just tol' ya that. And I also tol' ya ya need to get the fuck outa here. Now."

"Um, okay, I don't want no trouble. But can I please just put this back? Back where it belongs, I mean?" And he pointed off in the direction of court six.

"Ah, so you're the fuckin' dirtbag that stole the windscreen?"

"No, I ain't. I didn't take it."

"You didn't take it? You just happen to have it, and know where it came from and know what it's for. You're fulla shit, ain't ya, dirtbag?"

"No, Mister, I ain't. I ain't a liar and I didn't take it. I just wanna put it back."

He gathered up the windscreen and began inching forward without permission. This was a mistake. The man with the flashlight used his free hand to deliver a quick hard punch into Pineapple's solar plexus. The invisible blow knocked the air out of him and sent a spreading wave of pain up under his ribcage and down into his bowels. He doubled over and endured a long and fearful and puzzling moment of wondering if his lungs would ever fill again. When he got his breath back, he said, with a slight wheeze, and less in a tone of recrimination than of simple curiosity, "Why'd you do that, Mister? You didn't need to do that."

Was there just the faintest hint of remorse in the reply? "Needed to, no. Wanted to, yeah. Now just get the fuck outa here like I tol' ya inna first place."

"Okay, sure. But can I please just put this back?"

"Are you fuckin' deaf? I said get outa here."

"I carried it a long way, Mister. It's heavy."

"That's what ya get for stealin' it, dirtbag. Now get it outa here and get outa my face. Or do you wanna get hit again?"

Pineapple didn't, so he kept quiet and gingerly bent down to retrieve the windscreen once again. Unfurled and rumpled, it was impossible to lift entirely clear of the ground, so he half-carried and half-dragged it back toward the bleachers. When he judged that he'd put sufficient distance between himself and his attacker, he paused to roll the fabric up again.

Then he had a decision to make. Part of him wanted just to leave the goddamn windscreen right where it was. It had caused him enough trouble already, and maybe leaving it by the bleachers was good enough. But leaving it by the bleachers was not what he'd promised himself to do, and he hated to break a promise to himself. Plus, if he left the windscreen right there in the open, there was a pretty good chance, like the guy who hit him said, that someone would haul it away to sleep on, and then it would never find its way back to where it was meant to be, and maybe more people would get hurt on the court, and more ambulances would come, and now it would partly be his fault for falling short in finishing the job he'd started, and which he knew in his heart was the right thing to do.

So he lifted the heavy roll of fabric yet again, got it settled between the crook of his elbow and his hip, and, leaning parallel to the Higgs Beach palms, began the long walk home.

As he passed outside the courts where he had just had his misadventure, he suddenly heard the hard, dry pock of paddles and saw, through narrow gaps in the screens, what looked like the wiffle balls of his childhood, but mysteriously lighted from within, streaking back and forth across the net in low trajectories, leaving behind them a quickly dimming trail of greenish gleam, like shooting stars that fell to earth and stayed.

12.

The guest room door was closed when Pete got home. He leaned an ear against it and heard his mother peacefully snoring. So he went to the wine-and-music room, poured himself a Calvados, and put on a Faure quartet that never failed to calm him. Except that night it didn't work.

In the morning, after a fitful sleep filled with tatters of dreams that meandered from the absurd to the grotesque, he wolfed a cup of coffee and asked his mother for Gianni's cell number. She said, "So early you're calling? What if he's asleep?"

"He'll need to wake up. It's important."

She was wearing a pink robe and open-toe slippers with sprays of pink fluff at the insteps. She had just opened the refrigerator door and was standing sentinel in front of it, which gave her a commanding position of the crossroads between the fridge and the stove, which in turn gave her effective territorial control of the entire kitchen, which was the all-important first step toward annexing the whole house. She said, "But you haven't had your breakfast yet."

"I don't feel like breakfast, Mom."

"Not good for you, not having breakfast. Coffee by itself, it burns a hole right through your stomach."

"No it doesn't."

"Yes it does. I've seen it on TV. They show it. Right close up. Burns a hole right through. An ulcer. It can bleed. You should have some fiber, a little protein."

"I'm not hungry."

"Toast at least. A roll, a Danish. Something."

"Mom, I need to talk with Gianni and it might be better to do it on an empty stomach. So may I please just have the goddamn number?"

"Okay, okay. No need to get snippy about it."

In semi-voluntary exile, he took his phone outside and made the call from the porch. Penelope picked up. He hadn't been expecting that, and, badly rested and preoccupied as he was, he got thoroughly flustered and could not in that moment remember her name, a lapse for which he'd later be furious at himself. All he could manage was a rather tepid hello.

If his lack of enthusiasm hurt her feelings, she didn't let it show. "Oh, hi, Pete," she said. "Great to hear from you. How's it going?"

"Um, okay. Fine."

"You thought at all about some lessons? I'm just on my way out to teach a clinic. We could do a private right after if that works?"

"Um, I don't think so, thanks. Actually, I thought I was calling your uncle."

"You did. It's his line. I'm fielding calls for him. He's not getting around too well yet. Want me to put him on?"

"Nah, I need to talk him in person. Can I come by in five, ten minutes?"

"Yeah. Sure. Anytime."

"I don't know where you are," he said.

She gave him her address. Undaunted, she said, "If you change your mind about the lesson, I'll be at Higgs. Bring sneakers.

Expect a workout."

🌴 🌴 🌴

Penelope's place was down near the library, on a shady lane off Fleming Street. It was a modest addition to what had been a carriage house for a now divided larger home next door; but that was Key West, prices always going higher for spaces that kept shrinking on a patch of coral with nowhere to sprawl. Still, the miniature dwelling had a sort of munchkin charm to it, with yellow shutters on the windows and banks of bright red bougainvillea flanking the low door.

Pete knocked and Gianni hollered him in. He was wearing a green terry-cloth robe and leaning back against a rumpled pillow in what seemed to be the place's only armchair. His hurt leg in its blue-wrapped cast stretched across most of the living room, bisecting it on a neat diagonal before finding its perch on an upholstered stool.

"Make yourself comfortable," he said to his guest, apparently oblivious that his extended leg left only a couple of cramped triangles where anyone else might sit. Pete squeezed into a narrow chair just to the right of the hurt man's kneecap.

"So how's it goin'?" Gianni asked. "Any progress yet?"

By way of answer, Pete said, "There's a couple things I need to ask you, Gianni."

"Sure, Pete. Anything."

The visitor cleared his throat and suddenly realized he should have rehearsed. How did you just come right out and ask a person you hardly knew and who happened to be your mother's boyfriend if he used to be a Mafia stripper? He decided that an indirect approach might be the least embarrassing. "Secretariat," he said.

In response to Gianni's puzzled look, he added, "Mr. Ed."

The outside edges of Gianni's eyes narrowed just a fraction.

His Adam's apple shuttled up and down just once. "Yeah, what about 'em?"

"Seabiscuit. Seattle Slew. Trigger."

Gianni had olive skin with a Florida tan on top of it, but still a burgundy blush began to break through on his neck and forehead. "Where we goin' wit' this, Pete?"

"Horse, Gianni. Like, as a nickname. Gianni the Horse. Mean anything to you?"

He shifted the angle of his hurt leg a few degrees, frowned down at his chest, dragged the back of his hand across his lips and said, "Jesus Christ, you're an even more amazing detective than your mother says you are. How the hell'd you figure that out so fast?"

"Powers of deduction. Same way I gathered that your new apartment is 3F at the Paradiso Condominium."

"You found that out, too? Hardly anyone knows that. I haven't even told Gertie. Been savin' it for a surprise. Wanna see the look on her face when I open the curtain and show 'er the view. So come on, how'd you find out?"

Pete moved his narrow chair a couple of inches, which was about as far as it could go. "There's an older gentleman in town. From New York. A friend of friends of yours, as I believe the saying goes. Maybe you've heard of him. Bert d'Ambrosia."

"Bert d'Ambrosia? Bert the Shirt d'Ambrosia? Shit, course I heard of him. He's a legend. Big diplomat, peacemaker. Can't still be alive, though."

"Well, I grant you it's improbable. Except he is. And he lives on the fourth floor of the Paradiso. And he tells me you had a pretty good strip-tease act that the ladies just loved."

Gianni glared off at the only empty corner of the room. He tugged on an earlobe, scratched at his neck, and without looking back at Pete he said, "So you know about that too. I shoulda figured."

"Yeah, Gianni, I do. The nickname. The stripping. They sort of go together."

He slowly shook his head. "Oh well, I shoulda known I couldn't keep it a secret forever. Not once a real detective got involved."

"Real detective my eye. I spoke to Bert. Bert knew. That's it. But Gianni, you asked me to help you and then you gave me almost nothing to go on. Nada. Zip. Why the hell didn't you tell me?"

Gianni brought his eyes back across the room and gave his visitor a candid stare. "Well, for one thing, ya made it pretty clear ya didn't wanna know."

Pete felt an impulse to protest but realized that he had no grounds.

"And for another thing," the injured man went on, "I didn't want ya to judge me. I didn't want ya to think, this guy did certain things, that must mean he's a certain kinda person and always has been and always will be. Cause that's not the way it is, Pete. The stripping thing, I was young, I was broke, I had a neighborhood boss who pulled my strings. The strip club was something I did. It wasn't who I am. I need ya to believe that."

"I'm trying to believe it," said Pete. "I'd like to believe it. It's just a little tough thinking about my mother spending her sunset years with a guy who used to vamp around a stage with dollar bills sticking out of his underwear."

"That's a little harsh, Pete. I guess ya got a right to say it, but it's a little harsh. Look, think about the options I was lookin' at, where I came from, how little school I had. If I didn't fall into this strip club job I prob'ly woulda ended up a regular street thug. Would ya feel better if your mother was wit' someone like that? Someone who hurt people for a livin'? Someone who walked into a bar and people were afraid?"

Pete swallowed, fell short of holding Gianni's stare, and

looked down at a tiny patch of vacant floor.

"So look, ya can judge me or not, I got no control over that. But lemme tell ya the most important reason I was hopin' I wouldn't have to tell ya all this stuff. I just don't want it gettin' back to Gertie."

"Gertie doesn't know?"

"No way. I mean, how would she?"

"Well, she might've...um...noticed...I mean, the nickname and all..."

"Come on, Pete, the nickname was malarkey. I'm no stud muffin. Never was. It was a gig. But I'll tell ya this. It was a gig that made me think a little bit about how love's supposed to feel, 'cause it taught me plenty about how it doesn't feel. And I happen to be in love wit' your mother. And I don't want anything to change between her and me. If she got mad at me for things I did a million years ago, if it made her turn away...Look, maybe ya gotta be a certain age to see it this way, but I think there's maybe just a few times in life, very few, when ya have a chance to get it right on somethin' that you've always gotten wrong, and there comes a time when ya feel in your heart that this chance is the last best chance, and that if ya mess it up, you're done, it isn't comin' back. That's how I feel about Gertie. Does she feel that strong about me? If she does, I guess none a this other bullshit from way back when would matter. But I don't wanna risk it."

Pete stared out the only window he could see from his claustrophobic vantage next to Gianni's elevated leg. Outside, a ruby-throated hummingbird all but disappeared inside a red hibiscus bloom. A woodpecker blurred as it brained itself against a scabby palm. After a long pause he said, "You're putting me in a helluva position, Gianni."

"Yeah, I guess I am."

"She's my mother. I'm her son. She's staying at my house. So I'm supposed to get my mind around...let's call it her unconventional relationship, while at the same time miraculously helping solve your problem, which you still haven't really given me a handle on, and on top of that I'm supposed to keep it all a secret?"

"It's a lot t'ask," said Gianni. "I admit it."

"And you probably can't help much since your leg is in a cast."

"Nah, I'm not walkin' too good right now."

"And neither is my mother with her limp. And my only ally is about a hundred-fifty years old. And only yesterday I was sitting in my hot tub drinking Champagne and listening to Mozart and assuming that my mother was living a chaste and quiet and dignified widowhood in Jersey and everything seemed so simple. How the hell do I get roped into these things?"

"Never know what life's gonna throw at ya," said Gianni.

Pete lightly drummed his fingers against a thigh. "What about Penelope? Penelope know about your previous career?"

"She wasn't even born yet. Far as she knows, I'm just her uncle with the restaurant who mighta saved her life one time."

"Saved her life?"

Gianni dropped his voice and looked off to the side. "Look, she made a couple bad decisions. Ya know, the way kids do. Got herself in a dicey situation. Anyway, this was quite a few years ago and it's a whole 'nother story. Not really my place to talk about."

Pete said, "Okay, I get it. No gossip. But the strip club thing, it's supposed to be a secret from her, too?"

"Yeah, it is. Look, she looks up to me. I'd be embarrassed. Prob'ly she would, too."

Pete pressed his lips together and licked the inside of his teeth. "So let me make sure I have this right. You have a problem that seems to involve the Mafia. At some time in the past you were a stripper in a Mafia club. Maybe those two things go together, maybe they don't. And I'm supposed to connect the dots while hiding what might be the biggest dot from the two women who seem to be the people you're closest to in the whole wide world."

"Guess that's pretty much what it comes down to."

"Oh, for fuck's sake," said Pete, suddenly springing up from his chair without knowing that he was about to do so. Finding himself standing, he glanced left, glanced right, searching for somewhere he could pace and think, but there was no nowhere to go and so he sat back down again. "All right, all right," he said. "So fill me in about the strip club."

13.

"The third shot's the key," Penelope was saying to the eight students in her early clinic. "That's the shot that usually decides who's going to win the point. It should usually be short, low, angled to open up the middle. Got it?"

Seven of the eight people nodded. The eighth, a woman wearing one of those floppy bucket hats that go in and out of fashion but are fundamentally ridiculous, didn't nod but said she had a question. "Could you tell us about the scoring system one more time?"

Penelope kept a smile on her face but it took some effort. The goddamn scoring system. It was the bane of every pickleball instructor's life. It was complicated, it was confusing; for some students it was the hardest part of the game, and explaining it over and over again burned up court time that could have been so much better spent on stroke production, footwork, strategy. Nevertheless, Penelope explained it one more time, then said, "Okay, let's break up into foursomes and play some points."

The group fanned out across courts one and two, and soon the air was filled with the ugly yet cheering pock of balls rebounding off of paddles. It was the kind of perfect morning that people came to take for granted in the Keys—cool and moist, the barely moving breeze spiked with smells of salt and iodine, the sun still at a low angle that skidded beneath the brims of visors and made people pull their ball caps farther down across their eyes. Penelope glided from court to court, shortening a backswing here, coaxing out more of a follow-through there, reminding people to bend their knees, even though she knew that many of her students would go a lifetime without ever grasping the concept.

At some point a heavyset man in a Red Sox cap said, "Hey Teach, there's somethin' I been wonderin' about. That place you're not allowed to stand in. Why the heck's it called The Kitchen?"

"Well, no one seems to know for sure," Penelope admitted. "Might come from shuffleboard. Or it might just be that the people who invented the game wanted something less dorky than the No-Volley Zone. Everything's gotta be called something, right?"

She shrugged. A few people laughed. Then a voice came from the far side of court two. It was not a pleasant voice. It wasn't raspy, exactly, but there was something goading about it, an undertone of taunting. The voice belonged to a big man with broad shoulders and a thick neck. He had glistening black hair and was the only person on the courts who didn't wear a hat against the slanting sun. "I got a question, too," he said. "Whatcha doin' later, hon?"

Penelope looked sideways at him. Her lips kept smiling but her eyes did not. She was used to being flirted with and hit on, both on the court and off. It happened often enough that her radar had become quite finely honed as to the many shadings of intent and tone. She knew where the line was between charm and pushiness. She could tell a piece of innocent flattery from an insult in disguise. She had a feel for the frontier where mischief crossed over into creepiness. This advance was definitely on the creepy side. But she was a professional and she had seven other students who were there to have some fun and maybe learn a little, and she kept her answer very light and pleasant. "I'll be sitting quietly at home," she said, "with a tall iced tea and a very long book. Now let's get back to pickleball."

Play resumed. The big man without a hat didn't say another word for the entire session. Penelope noticed that he always swung hard even when a softer shot would have worked way better. He hit smashes right at people's hearts and faces. He played like a schoolyard bully and Penelope hoped he would never show up at the courts again.

14.

"So here's what went down," Gianni was saying. "I was twenty-three, twenty-four years old. Still lived where I was born, a fourth-floor walkup in what was still called Little Italy, even though most of the Italians had moved out by then and we were really more a part of Chinatown, which the old-timers weren't thrilled about, but that's life. We had a neighborhood boss. That was Paulie, the guy I already mentioned. Thing is, as the neighborhood got less important, so did Paulie. That's just how it works. Same wit' countries, right? You're head of a big county, ya got a lotta power. Dinky country, you're still the boss, but who cares? Anyway, what I'm tryin' to say is that Paulie was a big cheese for maybe a dozen blocks or so, but he also had guys from other neighborhoods, other Families, above him. Wanna beer?"

The question took Pete by surprise. It was around 9 am. He didn't want a beer. He heard himself say, "Yeah, sure, why not?"

Luxuriating in his helplessness, Gianni pointed over his shoulder toward the fridge. Pete squeezed past the injured man's heavy cast in its blue gauze wrapping and grabbed a couple cans. They were Budweisers. He handed one to Gianni and popped the other for himself. The opened can gave off a delicious-sounding hiss but the beer was all downhill from there. It didn't taste bad. It didn't taste good. Mostly it just didn't taste. Vaguely sweet, vaguely sour. It tasted like a damp coaster that someone had left sitting on a bar.

"Salud," said Gianni, then took a swig. "So anyway, I'm just gettin' to the age where I realize I gotta make a livin', so who do I go to for work? Paulie, of course. I dress up sharp and go to the place on Mulberry Street where he always takes his espresso. I ask permission to sit down in his booth. We talk. I'm tryin' to sound tough, even though I know deep down I'm not. And Paulie, let's give the man some credit here, he figures that out in about two minutes. These old bosses could see right through guys. They were like part priest, part shrink. Okay, part killers too. No one's perfect. But anyway, I can tell he's got me pegged but he doesn't wanna trash my ego. So he tells me that he doesn't have any openings just then for protection or collection work, but he's got this little club—"

"The strip club," Pete put in.

"Yeah. On a little side-street offa Chambers, a few blocks from where the Trade Center useta be. Seemed like it would be a good location, like for business guys who wanted to have a coupla pops and a little stimulation before catchin' a later train and tellin' their wives they were stuck at work. Except it wasn't workin' out. Too much competition innee other boroughs and even out inna suburbs. So Paulie tells me he's got practically nothin' left to lose onna place, and he'd be willin' to gimme a shot at helpin' to run it for six months or so to see if I could turn it around or at least make it pay for itself. If it worked out, great. If not, maybe he'd have somethin' else for me by then. But he knew and I knew that the somethin' else would be a tough guy gig, and we both knew I'd be bad at it. So I was pretty whaddyacallit, motivated, to make the club thing work."

He paused for a pull of beer. Pete pretended to be drinking some of his and looked forward to an opportunity to pour the rest of it discreetly down the sink.

"So I start as a bartender and get to know the place. It's a pretty crummy joint. There's a stage wit' some red and blue and purple lights. There's an old piano that's outa tune and no one ever plays it, so the music just comes through these dusty speakers that buzz. The strippers come and go. Some of 'em used to dance in better places but are past their prime. Some are kids workin' their way through college. But the tips are lousy and there's only so much the club can pay 'em, so they don't stick around for long. As for the customers, yeah, we get some businessmen, sometimes wit' clients from outa town who get a charge outa hangin' out in Sin City wit' mostly naked women. Just not enough of those guys. Then we get goombahs from other neighborhoods who maybe tip the girls okay 'cause they wanna look like bigshots, but expect to get their drinks for free. Bottom line, the place ain't makin' money.

"Long story short, a coupla months go by, the manager quits, so now it's on me. The clock is tickin'. I only got so much time to make it work or else Paulie's gonna put a gun or a baseball bat in my hand and send me inta combat. So I'm nervous. Depressed even. I start takin' long walks through the neighborhood, just tryin' to keep my head straight, maybe come up wit' some bright idea. Then one day it hits me. Those big office buildin's all around, who's mostly comin' out of 'em at five, five-thirty innee afternoon? Not guys. Not mostly. It's women. Thousands o' women. They come streamin' out in twos and threes, chattin' wit' their girlfriends while they're walkin' to the subway, which takes them like half a block from where the club is. So suddenly it seems so obvious. Ladies Night! Ladies Night is gonna save my ass.

"'Course," he went on, "I have no idea how to get it started. So I talk to this woman Bebe, one a the older strippers who still shows up. Very smart, lots of experience. I ask her how to hire a guy stripper. She says, 'Don't.' I say, 'Don't?' She says, 'Don't. They're hard to find, plus they're usually unreliable divas. Everything's a freakin' drama and then when you have to fire 'em ya have a whole big scene on your hands. Why not just do it yourself?'

"Well, I seem to remember I was drinkin' a Seven-and-Seven at the time, and I spit it out all over the bar. Before I can talk again, she says, 'Why not? You're here anyway. No one extra to hire or fire. No extra overhead. You'd need a stage name.' She looks me up and down like I'm hangin' inna butcher shop window, and she says 'The Horse. Gianni the Horse. That's not bad. So here's what we'll do. We'll take a photo, get some flyers printed up, staple 'em all over the neighborhood...'

"So this is movin' way too fast for me and I just say to Bebe, 'Whoa, slow down.' Except she doesn't. She just grabs a piece a paper and writes down an address. 'Leather shop up inna Village,' she says. 'They'll have everything ya need.'

"I'm thinkin', leather shop, yeah right, like that's ever gonna happen. An' I stick the piece a paper in my pocket an' more a less forget about it. Coupla days go by, I'm lookin' at my empty club, dealin' wit' the liquor guy who's gettin' antsy to get paid...Long story short, I go to the leather joint.

"There's a very tall guy behind the counter. Shaved head. Pierced eyebrows. Tats all over his neck. Very friendly guy. He asks how he can help. I really don't know what t'ask for, so I just say I need a coupla outfits. He says he's sure he can satisfy my needs and he asks me top or bottom.

"I tell him it's mainly the bottom part I'd like to cover up.

"He says, 'Sorry, I'm asking if you're a top or bottom.'

"I say, 'Huh?'

"He says, 'Dom or sub?'

"I say, 'Look, I don't go in for any a that kinky stuff.'"

"'No?' he says. 'Then why are you here?'

"I lower my voice and say, 'Cause I wanna be a stripper.'

"'Ah,' he says and he smiles. 'No value judgment, but wouldn't you say that qualifies as kinky?'

"I say, 'Look, it's not that I wanna be a stripper, it's that I gotta be a stripper.'

"'I understand,' he says. 'These urges run very deep. Why even try to resist?'

"'Look,' I say, 'it's not a fuckin' urge, it's business. Can I please just get a coupla outfits?'"

Gianni drained his Bud and crumpled the can. "Want another beer?"

Pete did not want another beer. He didn't even want the one he already had in front of him. But he went to the fridge to fetch Gianni a fresh one. Reaching in, he could immediately tell which shelf Penelope had reserved for herself. It held yogurt, cottage cheese, celery sticks, alfalfa sprouts, and those adorable baby carrots that were hardly bigger than ear plugs. No wonder women outlived men.

"So anyway, long story short," Gianni went on, "I get the outfits. One's like a bib thing, like wrestlers wear, one's just a glorified jockstrap. I bring 'em down to the club. Bebe tells me to put 'em on. I'm, like, dyin' a thousand deaths, but I do it. She takes a picture, gets a flyer printed up, and suddenly I'm plastered all over downtown three-quarters naked, hopin' that no one I actually know will ever see it.

"Then it's Tuesday, the first Ladies Night. The crowd's so-so, but already better'n we usually do wit' the deadbeat guys. It gets to be my time to go on. And I can't do it. I'm standin' behind the curtain at the edge of the little stage, and I can't get my legs to move. The music's playin' but I can't pick up the beat. I'm in a cold sweat. The audience starts gettin' antsy, a few people slappin' onna tables. So what happens? Bebe comes up behind me and pinches me onnee ass. I don't mean a little pinch like you give a baby's cheek. I mean a pinch that hurts. An' she gives me a little push and she says, 'Get out there and enjoy it.'

"So the pinch sorta gets me over the hump, and I walk out on stage, and gradually I loosen up and start to move a little, and I'm lookin' out at the audience and everybody looks like they're havin' fun, and at some point I realize, holy shit, so am I. I mean, it's a goof. People look happy. No one's gettin' hurt. So I ease into a dance and get out among the tables, and I finish my number and everybody's clappin'. Who doesn't like bein' clapped for, right?

"Anyway, long story short, Ladies Night takes off. Women tell their friends. The next Tuesday, there's like twice as many people. Tuesday after that, we're bringin' in more tables. Within a couple months, it's standin' room only. And that's when the trouble starts."

"Cops?" said Pete. "Fire regulations?"

"Nah, nuthin' like that. Paulie had those guys paid off for years. The problem was wit' the goombahs who used to come in and act like bigshots before we changed the format. They had this attitude, like the best tables were just automatically theirs. They were used ta havin' the waitresses and strippers fall all over 'em. Suddenly it wasn't that way no more. Now the place was full and they didn't count for much. That's what they were mad at. That they didn't get treated like bigshots. 'Cept of course they wouldn't admit that's what it was, so they found somethin' else to get pissed off about. Namely, that once the word got out about Ladies Night, it wasn't only ladies that came in. Women sometimes brought friends who happened to be guys. Guys started bringin' other guys. So it got to be a very mixed crowd that had a really nice feel to it wit' no hassles and people havin' a lotta laughs and spendin' money. Just a buncha different kinds a people relaxin' wit' some drinks and a goofball male stripper, namely me."

"So finally there comes a Tuesday when the place is packed and this group of six or seven knuckleheads from Brooklyn are squeezed into a kinda crummy table up against the wall. This guy Freddy, who's kinda the leader of the pack, calls me over. So I go. It's parta the job, right? Well, it's pretty obvious that he's had quite a few drinks that he doesn't plan on payin' for anyway, and it's pretty obvious he's playin' to his buddies, and he says to me, loud enough for half the room to hear, 'Hey Gianni, what the hell you doin' runnin' a fag joint.'

"So I say to him, 'Freddy, I don't like that kinda talk.'

"And he says, 'No? But ya like waggin' your dick around in a roomful a homos?'

"So I say, 'Look, this is a public establishment. Everybody's welcome here, unless they act like a fuckin' asshole.'

"So he seems to think this over for a couple seconds, like maybe he can't quite figure it out wit' all the booze in 'im. Then he says, 'Did you just call me an asshole?'

"I just shrug. I mean, why say it twice? But the damage is done. He's insulted and he isn't gonna let it go. 'You got a lotta fuckin' nerve,' he says, 'dissin' me in a club fulla queers.'

"Well, that about does it for me. I say, 'Freddy, I'm very sorry that you don't seem to like my little place no more. Maybe there's another club nearby that would suit you better.'

"'You kickin' me out?' he says. 'You got the fuckin' balls to eighty-six me from this dump? Well, you can't kick me out. We're leavin'. Come on, guys.'

"So they get up from the table, knockin' over a coupla chairs as they go, no mention a coverin' the tab of course. Then Freddy reaches into his pocket, takes out a buncha change and throws it onna floor. 'An' that's what I think a your limpdick strip show,' he says.

"They go stompin' out, throwin' some elbows here and there, and that was pretty much it," said Gianni. "That was the beginning of the end of my club."

He sucked some beer and glanced at his watch. "Shit, I'm due for a pill. Would ya mind grabbin' 'em for me? They're onna nightstand next to the bed."

Pete stood up, maneuvered around the hurt man's armchair, and went into the only bedroom the little cottage had, Penelope's bedroom. She'd given her uncle the use of it while she herself had been sleeping on a sofa; but still, it was her bedroom, and Pete felt a fleeting illicit tingle, a hint of stolen intimacy as he stepped into the room. The walls were painted pale peach. The louvered window threw softly writhing stripes of light and shadow across the vacant bed. There didn't seem to be a closet; Penelope's featherweight blouses and sundresses hung on a wooden pole suspended from the ceiling; the slightest scrap of breeze sent them dancing. Pete was tempted to touch the garments but his conscience didn't let him. He allowed himself a deep and slightly guilty breath before picking up the pill bottle.

Handing it to Gianni, he said, "So what happened with the club?"

The injured man shook out a pill, washed it down with beer, and said, "Well, here's what I think musta happened. I think Freddy and those other knuckleheads musta gone back to their bosses, who were higher up the food chain from where Paulie was, and given them some bullshit version a what happened, and made it sound like I insulted them and threw them out, and prob'ly made a big deal about the gay thing and how it wasn't right and what an embarrassment it was that one of their own people, an Italian guy from Little Italy, should be strippin' for an audience that had men in it along wit' women, and they prob'ly turned it into this whole crazy macho thing like I'm a threat to the masculinity of the whole organization 'cause I'm out in public in a jockstrap. So I think those bosses musta bought the story and put the screws to Paulie, and Paulie put the screws to me, and that was the end of the strip club, just when it was finally startin' to turn some cash."

He gave a resigned shrug and followed it up with a long pull of his Bud. Then he said, "And, who knows, maybe that was the start of this whole mysterious grudge and even the root a the problem I got now."

"You think so?" said Pete. "I mean, that was, like, almost forty years ago, right? You think someone's holding a grudge over something that happened in a strip club forty years ago?"

"Who knows? Guys get crazy over this masculinity stuff. Guys get all worked up. And who gets worked up the most? The guys who hate the show 'cause, deep down, they're scared shitless that maybe they really like the show. Who knows?"

Pete thought that over while pretending to take a sip of his warm and sour beer. Could Gianni's problem really have come from some macho goombah's flash of homosexual panic half a lifetime ago? It would be lunacy but that didn't mean it couldn't happen. It would not be unprecedented, after all, for one man to kill another rather than admit he was in love with him.

But just as this theory was picking up momentum in Pete's mind, Gianni said casually, "Then again, maybe it don't have nothin' to do with that. Maybe it's more to do with the restaurant."

Pete rubbed his eyes. "But you told me everything was copacetic with the restaurant. That's the exact word you used. Stuck in my mind."

"Yeah, I said that. But I only heard it from Mort, and maybe Mort's lyin'. I mean, he's from Paramus."

"This makes him a liar?"

"Well, it don't make 'im Abe Lincoln. Maybe he's got an angle of his own. Maybe he's coverin' up for someone."

"Like who?"

"Well, I dunno, 'cause since Paulie died I don't know who really owns my restaurant. Maybe it's the same Brooklyn honchos who had the leverage to make Paulie close the club. It's tough to know. These guys don't write stuff down. Maybe there's a beef that just comes down to money."

Pete scratched the back of his neck. That made him realize his nose itched so he scratched that too. "Gianni," he said, "you're driving me crazy. First you take me on a roller-coaster ride about strip clubs and leather jocks and crazy macho homophobia, now you tell me it just comes down to a business dispute. So which is it?"

Seeing Pete scratch his nose made Gianni realize that his forehead itched, so he gave it a scratch before saying, "Who knows? Could be either. Could be both. Could be somethin' different altogether."

"Well, that clears it up."

"I guess not really. Sorry. But one thing's for sure. Wherever the stupid grudge came from, why's it croppin' up now? I gotta believe it's croppin' up 'cause Paulie died, and his kickin' the bucket means that after all these years I ain't under his protection no more.

Which means the on'y protection I got right now is you."

Pete shuffled his feet and swallowed. His saliva tasted more sour than the nasty beer.

"Other'n'at, my friend, I'm as exposed as I was that first time when I was sweatin' bullets and walked out onna stage. 'Cept this time no one's clappin'."

15.

Exasperated and bewildered, Pete got home to find Gertie floating face down in the pool, one arm stretched motionless in front of her as if grasping at eternity, her rings cruelly glinting in the sunlight, the short skirt of her old-lady bathing suit bobbing limply on the lightly rippled surface.

"Mom!" he yelled. "Mom!" And he jumped in with his clothes on to try to save her.

By the time his sneakers hit the water, she'd rolled over and was doing the backstroke.

"Mom," he screamed, reaching for her arm. "Jesus Christ, I thought you were dead. I thought you drowned."

"Drowned?" she said. "Who could drown in a pool this size? My feet touch bottom. Practically before I kick I'm at the other side."

Standing now, she blinked the chlorine out of her eyes, took a closer look at her son, and went on. "And you? You go in with your clothes on? In the hot tub you go naked, in the pool you wear clothes? I'm getting a little worried about you, Peter. You didn't act this way when you lived in Jersey. Does everybody act this way down here?"

"Mom, I jumped in because—"

"Look, you don't need to explain. It's your house, it's your pool, I'm not here to tell you how to live your life. You're more comfortable with shoes on, fine. How's Gianni?"

He didn't get to answer because just then the doorbell rang.

This was quite unusual. Hardly anybody ever came to visit Pete, and those few who did, his mother for example, tended to be more the types who barged right in. Curious, he dragged himself out of the pool. Water was streaming from his sneakers. His shirt was plastered to his chest and armpits. His khaki shorts were saturated and rivulets were chasing one another down his legs. A bead of water followed him as he made his way through the house and opened the front door.

Penelope was standing there, her skin glowing from her morning in the sunshine, her muscles taut from demonstrating proper form, her black hair clasped just so beneath her visor. She said, "Oh, hi, Pete, I hope you don't mind but..." She stopped herself, glanced at him a moment with her violet eyes, then said, "Um, you're wet."

He looked down at the little puddles still oozing from his sneakers and thought Why do I always have to look, sound, feel, and act like an idiot when she's around? He said, "Oh, yeah, right. I was in the pool."

She just looked at him and he felt a moronic but irresistible impulse to go on.

"My mother. I thought she was drowning."

"Drowning?"

"Well, she wasn't. She was swimming. Slowly. It was my mistake. I guess I've been a little overwrought the last couple days."

"Well, who could blame you?" said Penelope, at which point Pete realized he was compounding his idiocy by leaving her just standing in the doorway as if she was a Jehovah's Witness pushing leaflets.

"But come in," he said, "come in. Careful, the floor's a little damp."

He led her through the house. She took quick looks at the

mismatched furniture and the eccentric paintings on the walls—here a Haitian village scene, there a thrown-paint abstract. When they got back out to the pool, they found Gertie standing in the shallow end doing PT stretches for her artificial hip. She sang out a hello to the younger woman and asked her how her class went.

"Actually," said Penelope, "it was pretty disturbing. That's why I came right over. Right after I spoke with Uncle Gianni, I mean. Mind if I sit a minute?"

Pete gestured her toward a chair. The way she settled into it was part poetry, part magic trick, a vision of the sort of everyday gracefulness that some few people have and is so quiet and compact that it usually goes unnoticed. She didn't use her arms at all. She just folded her body into the shape of the chair and descended softly into it as if gravity had been suspended.

"So what happened?" Gertie asked her, continuing to swing her repaired hip in little circles.

"Well, there was a guy in the clinic. Very unpleasant. Very inappropriate. I was upset when I got home, so I told Uncle Gianni about it, and from the way I described him, Gianni thinks it's the same guy who's been stalking him, who made him fall down on the court."

Pete cupped his chin in his hand and said, "Hmm. Was this guy by any chance the only person in the clinic who didn't wear a hat?"

Penelope pursed her lips adorably while she thought that over. "I think that's right. I think that's exactly right. He had black hair and he didn't wear a hat. Wow. How'd you even know that?"

"Just a hunch."

"Just a hunch," echoed Gertie. "You see how modest he is? He knew because he's brilliant."

Pete started to protest then decided to let the preposterous comment stand. Maybe it would balance out the imbecilic image of him standing there in sopping clothes and squishing shoes and acting like it was only normal. Better to be regarded as an idiot savant than just an idiot.

"Anyway," Penelope resumed, "this guy just seemed like a bully and a creep. Like someone, I don't know, like someone you might see smoking in the shadows on a street corner or maybe wobbling out of a strip club somewhere."

That last phrase hung in the chlorine-laden air for a second or two, and Pete said, a little weakly, "And that would mean he was an awful person? Just automatically, I mean? That he went to a strip club? That would be enough?"

"Well, it wouldn't recommend him as a dating prospect."

Gertie continued with her exercise, then said with a giggle, "Oh, I don't know. I was in a strip club once."

Her son said, "You were? You never told me that."

"Like I have to tell you everything?"

"And you didn't mind?" asked Penelope. "The stripping, I mean."

"Mind? I thought it was a riot. The one I went to, it was guys. The strippers. Big young men."

"Sounds a little gross," said Penelope.

"Well, it wasn't. No offense, but I think maybe you younger people have gotten a little prudish lately. This was just fun. Chippendale's, the place was called. Had guys dressed up sort of like Playboy bunnies. Big bow-ties and not much else. Nice switch from always having the women be gawked at. It was hilarious. We laughed about it for years."

"You and Dad?" asked Pete.

"That stick in the mud? No, no way. Not that he wasn't a prince of a man. But this was me and the Mah Jongg ladies. We were in the City for a matinee. Sound of Music, I think it was. Such a beautiful show. So inspiring."

"Such a perfect warm-up for a strip club," Pete put in.

"Okay, be sarcastic," said his mother. "It happens to be a very nice memory." She continued with her water exercises, then after a moment or two went on. "But you know what? If you two don't mind, please let's not tell Gianni that story."

"Oh come on, Mom. You think he'd care in the least?"

"Well, I don't know. Probably not. But he's such a gentleman. So respectful. Really pretty strait-laced. Why take a chance on making him uncomfortable?"

Penelope said, "Yeah, pretty hard to imagine Uncle Gianni getting anywhere near a strip club. He'd probably blush and cross the street." She gave Gertie a wink. "So let's just keep this our little secret."

Pete rocked in his sopping shoes. Our little secret. It was getting tougher by the minute to keep track of what he was supposed to hide from whom.

Gertie said, "But you were telling us about the creep in class…"

"Right," said Penelope. "That guy. Well, I noticed a couple of things about him that might help us figure out what his deal is."

She turned a candid gaze on Pete, assuming that the detective would be on high alert for receiving any clues. But at that instant, what he was actually wondering about was how long it would take to develop athlete's foot from standing in wet shoes. Belatedly, he refocused his attention and, a fraction off the beat, said, "Um, like what?"

"Well, for one thing, he has a nice car. Not a limousine, but close. Jersey plate—"

Shaking her head, Gertie put in, "Jersey plate. This already I don't like."

"—and he keeps it parked on that little street behind the courts. Fits nice and snug between two No Overnight Parking signs."

Pete said, "Those signs don't count for much down here."

"Or maybe," Gertie said, "this is a type of person your local cops would rather not annoy."

"Mom, are you suggesting that Key West's finest would shrink from taking on the Mafia?"

To Penelope, the old lady said, "You see, there he goes again with the sarcasm. You just have to expect it. I don't think he can help himself."

"Well, anyway," Penelope went on, "I've noticed the car parked there for at least a couple days now. It's there first thing in the morning. It's there last thing when I leave at night. I think the guy's been sleeping in it."

Pete said, "Or maybe he just keeps it parked there."

"Well, after the clinic this morning, I watched him leave the court. I kept my distance but I followed on my bike."

"You tailed him?" Gertie said excitedly. "Look who's being the detective now!"

The young woman gave a modest shrug. "I was just hoping to help. Anyway, he opens up a back door, and I see a pillow and a blanket still laid out. And then I noticed something else I thought was really interesting."

Gertie said, "What? What?"

Pete was trying to kick off his sneakers but the canvas had

swelled and they wouldn't budge.

"I saw a big bag of those special pickleballs that light up at night."

A look of anticlimax sneaked across Gertie's face. Pete's expression was more one of utter incomprehension.

After a moment, Penelope went on. "Don't you see? You can't play pickleball alone, and this place empties out as soon as the lights go off. So he has these special balls for nighttime. Which maybe means that someone comes out to play with him. Maybe someone who doesn't want to be seen in daylight."

Pete thought that over while trying not to obsess on the fact or fantasy that his toes were already starting to itch. "Well, just because the guy has light-up balls doesn't mean he has a nighttime game or that it would connect to anything."

Gertie said, "I don't hear you coming up with anything better, Mr. Smarty."

Penelope said, "Look, maybe it means nothing. But we know for sure this guy hangs around the courts a lot. And it could only help if we found out whether he had a buddy or a boss or whatever. And it just seems like pickleball's the way to do that. Maybe you'd even end up in a game with him sometime."

"Me?" said Pete.

"Who else?" said his mother.

"I've never touched a paddle in my life."

"Which is why I was thinking we'd start your lessons this evening," said Penelope.

"Look, I never agreed—"

"We'll start at dusk," the lovely instructor went on. "Two birds, one stone. If the guy happens to be out there playing, that's a bonus. If not, you'll be learning the game so you'll be ready for whatever happens next."

"Whatever happens next?"

"So let's say 8 o'clock," Penelope said blithely. "We'll have the last of the lighted time and then we'll see if anything goes on in the dark."

16.

"That's bullshit!" said Fred, when, late the next morning, he'd noticed that the pilfered windscreen was once again leaning against the hot dog wagon and had heard Piney's account of his failed mission to the Higgs Beach courts. "That's total bullshit, the way he talked to you. Fuck gives him the right to talk like that?"

Piney was whittling a piece of driftwood into a shape more or less like a dolphin. Without looking up, he said, "Can't help how people talk. People wanna call me names, I guess they can. Mostly rolls right off. Mostly. Bugs me a little bit sometimes. Doesn't matter."

"Matters to me," said Fred, "and I say it's bullshit. And he hit you? Why the hell'd he hit you?"

"Guess you'd have to ask him that. Guess he didn't like my talkin' back 'stead of just leavin' like he told me to."

"And who the hell's he to be tellin' you to leave? Place is a public park."

"That's what I thought, too," said Piney, continuing to whittle. He was working on the snout, trying to shape the slightly undercut jaw that made dolphins look like they were always smiling.

"How big was he?" asked Fred.

"I have no idea. I never saw much of him. He had this really bright light, from a phone I guess. I saw the light, I felt the punch, that was pretty much it."

"Well, it's bullshit and it pisses me off and next time I'm goin' with you."

Piney lifted the knife from the evolving little sculpture. He didn't like to stop in the middle of something he was doing; he felt there was a momentum or a flow or something he just didn't have a word for that slipped away and was tough to find again if he broke his concentration; but he thought his buddy's comment needed answering right away. "Um, Fred, I don't think that's such a good idea."

The objection came too late and probably didn't matter anyway. Fred was already committed to the notion. "He gives us any trouble, I go low, you go high, we take him down."

"Well, then what? Maybe we hurt him. Maybe he hurts us. Maybe everyone hurts everybody. Maybe the cops come and we're standing there and everybody's bleeding and we're holding the windscreen and how do we get out of that one? I'm just not sure I see the point of fighting."

Fred stomped over to a good-sized coral rock and kicked it. "The point is that sometimes ya just gotta stand up for what's right."

"Well, that's what I was tryin' to do bringin' the stupid windscreen back. All it got me is the wind knocked outa me. But I'll try again. I'll pick a different night, a different time. I'll get it done."

"We're doin' it together," said Fred, with his jaw pushed out and his eyes narrowed down, a familiar expression that told Pineapple very clearly that he wasn't going to change his mind and it would be a waste of breath to argue.

So the tall man just shrugged and went back to his whittling. Sure enough, though, the half-minute of distraction had cost him the feel for what he'd been doing. The little piece of driftwood in his hand no longer looked much like a dolphin, he decided. It no longer felt to him like it wanted to become a dolphin. It just looked and felt like a bleached and curvy stick with some scratch marks on it. He tossed it aside. It would make good kindling for that evening's campfire.

17.

"I don't usually drink before I teach," said Penelope.

"Sound policy," said Pete. "But I can't learn a new sport on an empty stomach, and I find that oysters go down way better with a glass of wine, so I'm having a dozen raw and a small carafe of Muscadet. Let your conscience be your guide."

She perched her chin on her fist and thought about it, but not for long. "My conscience tells me there's no way I could sit across from someone slurping oysters and not want to have some. I'll take a dozen, too. And maybe just one glass of wine."

They were sitting in the courtyard at Raoul's, one of the increasingly rare fixed points in the transient and swirling pocket-size universe of Key West. Year after year, decade after decade, Raoul's stayed the same. The same scabby mahogany tree soared up through an opening in the tin roof, its leaves and seed pods lightly scraping against the metal and sounding very like a snare drum played with brushes. The same unfussy, trend-free offerings stayed on the menu; they still did Thanksgiving dinner every single Thursday night. The cocktail sauce was still coarse-cut and unlike any other. The owner still sat at the bar and had a bowl of corn flakes every night at closing time to save himself the trouble of breakfasting next day.

A server came over to take their order. When it got to the part about a small carafe and a single glass of Muscadet, she said, "Might be a better deal just to get a liter."

This struck Pete as eminently reasonable and he shot a questioning glance across the table. Penelope shrugged with her eyebrows alone and consented with just the slightest tip of her head. "'S'gonna be a wobbly lesson," she said.

"So I'll have an excuse if I mess up," said Pete.

"You won't mess up. Not if you're anything like the athlete your mother says you are."

"Oh Christ, that again. Except I'm not. According to my mother, I won Wimbledon, scored a touchdown at the Super Bowl, and could hit a home run with a breadstick."

"It's nice that she's so proud of you."

"I guess. So why is it that nothing I do is exactly right? I bring her dinner, there's no vegetables. I jump in the pool to save her from drowning, she thinks it's weird I have my shoes on."

"Family," she said. "It's always complicated, right? The more they love you, the more they drive you crazy. And if they don't love you enough, that drives you crazy, too."

"So which was it for you?" said Pete, and instantly regretted the question. "No, sorry, that's way too personal. Didn't mean to pry."

"Hey, you're a detective."

Weary of denying it, he just looked down at his hands.

"I guess probably a little bit of both," she went on. "I wouldn't call it the happiest story."

She was spared from saying more just then by the arrival of the wine. The big carafe was frosty. There was a barely audible glug full of expectation as the server poured. They clinked glasses. A nice custom and, for such a simple gesture, admitting of such a range of nuance. Strangers at bars clink glasses; it means nothing. Conventioneers who can't stand each other clink glasses at banquets; it means less than nothing. But when two unattached people clink across a small table on a sultry evening with the languorous smell of the ocean never far away, and their eyes lock, if only for the briefest interval, so that the rest of the world becomes an indifferent blur at the edges of their vision, and if they hold that gaze for even a fraction of a second longer than it takes for their glasses to kiss and retreat...well, then a clink means...then it means whatever the co-conspirators in the gesture want it to or hope it will.

After the first sip, Penelope said, "Oh boy, that's crisp."

"Classic oyster wine," said Pete, and with some effort managed to stop himself from going off into the kind of cork-dork tangent that generally bored other people to death.

Unaware that she'd just been spared a long spiel about soil types and microclimates, Penelope said, "Nice of Gertie to offer to make dinner for Uncle Gianni. I hope he's okay with it. He's used to being in charge in the kitchen."

"So's she. Anybody's kitchen."

"You think she did it so they could be alone, or so we could be?"

"I actually hadn't thought about it that way," said Pete, thereby revealing one of the age-old differences between women and men. "But I guess it's sort of like a double-date except we don't actually have to be around each other...But you were starting to tell me about your family."

"I was?" Her eyes slid away from his, then worked their way back. "Well, okay, here's the very short version. Mom was a tough cookie. Very Catholic, very strict. Long on rules, short on affection. Dad was a sweetheart who also happened to be a total screwup. Drank too much, went from job to job, really bad with money. She was always finding fault with him, big faults, little faults, and I don't blame her. He got sick of it and left one day, and I don't blame him either. Why blame anybody? I mean, I guess everybody could blame everybody for everything, but where does it get you?"

The question was still hanging when the oysters appeared, their shells rattling softly in their ice-filled trays as the server set them down, the promised savor of the present moment washing away some of the bad taste of the past.

They clinked glasses once again, this time as people who had gotten to know each other just a tiny bit better. Penelope pinned Pete with her violet eyes and said, "Anyway, thanks for listening."

"Thanks for talking."

They started in, daintily lifting the half-shells to their lips, tipping them forward to get the first delicious trickle of icy brine, then teasing out the flesh with gentle tugs of the teeth and patient probing of the tongue before committing to the plump and sweet and mouth-filling swallow. They watched each other do this. How could they not? Should they look down and go cross-eyed? Look away and spill the brine? So their gazes skated along the plane of each other's lips, the pleasure of eating oysters amplified by the pleasure of seeing oysters being coaxed and nibbled across the narrow table.

During a break for a sip of wine, Penelope, more relaxed now, said, "But I didn't get to the happy part of the story."

"Hm?"

"My family. The happy part. The loving part. That'd be Uncle Gianni. After my Dad left, he really stepped up. Would take me to movies, shows, ballgames, skating in Rockefeller Center. I mean, he was a pal. Really kind of father and mother both, since Mom started spending most of her time in church, except when she was home giving me nasty looks for not going to Mass with her."

"So he never had kids of his own?"

"No kids. Never married. Had girlfriends now and then. Never seemed to get serious. Said he was too busy with the restaurant. Besides, he was basically a stay-at-home guy. I think he'd always been like that."

Except for a brief career as a stripper, thought Pete.

They went back to the many-sided pleasure of eating oysters, their eyes on one another's lips.

When the platters were empty except for the vacant shells

and some shrinking islands of melting ice, and the carafe of wine was down to its last two finger-widths of Muscadet, Pete said, "It's nice that you're so devoted to him. Especially now that he's in trouble, I mean."

She sipped some wine. She'd mostly stuck to her pledge of having just one glass. Not entirely. Very softly, she said, "Well, the shoe's been on the other foot."

"Meaning?"

"It doesn't really matter. Long time ago. I made some very bad choices. Maybe rebellious. Sticking it to Mom. Maybe just dumb. Anyway, he saw me through, cleaned up a mess I'd made. Could've been really bad."

She fell silent, looked down at nothing in particular. Pete honored the moment by leaving his wine glass alone though he would have liked to have another swallow.

Some seconds passed, then she reached out a hand toward one of his. For just an instant he imagined she was about to clasp his fingers in a lover's gentle but emphatic grip and offer up some intimate confession. But all she did, in fact, was tap him lightly on the knuckles and, managing a smile, said, "Come on, let's go play some pickleball."

18.

There was still a bit of color in the western sky, just a dim veil of pinkish lavender dangling close to the horizon, when they climbed off their bikes at the Higgs Beach courts. The daytime breeze had dropped and, across the street, the barely rippled ocean offered up a coppery reflection. There was no sound of crashing surf, just the soft sizzle of foam subsiding through pebbles at the water's edge.

The court lights were on but no one was playing at that hour. Penelope pulled a couple of paddles and some balls out of her backpack, then did a few effortless stretches against the bleachers before suggesting they hit a few back and forth just to loosen up. Pete took a paddle and went to the far side of the court. He was surprised to find that the paddle weighed almost nothing. The net was much lower than a tennis net. Two steps in any direction would take you anywhere you might need to get to. This was going to be an easy game.

He came forward onto the balls of his feet and rocked into a ready position. The beautiful instructor sent a soft and lofted shot toward his forehand. He whiffed and watched the ball roll to the fence.

"Shit, that's embarrassing. Must be the wine."

"Probably not," she said. "It's that your brain imagines that the paddle is the same length as a racket. Commonest mistake when people come over from tennis. Just try turning off the muscle memory and watch the ball. You'll get it."

And, allowing for a handful of muffs and mishits, he did. Within a few minutes they were rallying gently but fairly consistently from mid-court, when Penelope said, "Okay, you're doing fine, but there's one more tennis habit you're going to have to break. Your swing is too big. Too much take-back. Too much follow-through. It's a small court. You'll be sharing it with a partner. You swing like that, you'll clobber someone."

So Pete tried swinging more compactly. To Penelope's practiced eye, it wasn't working.

She said, "Here, let me show you," and she walked with her unself-conscious grace through the veil of twilight toward his side of the court. Casually resting her own paddle against the net post, she stepped behind him, and said, "Mind if I touch you? I promise it won't hurt a bit."

"Um, no, I don't mind," said Pete, as she was already reaching out to grasp the wrist of his hand that held the paddle. Firmly, she coaxed his elbow closer to his ribs then swiveled to her right, tugging him in parallel. Her chest was against his shoulder blades. Her tummy breathed in and out against his back. Their hips pivoted together, synchronized.

He felt her breath against his neck as she said softly, "See? That's the way it starts. That's all the movement you need. Nothing more than that. Got it?"

"Um, not really. I don't think so. Maybe show me one more time? A little slower, maybe?"

They did the dance again, spooned, swaying together, holding the final pose as if it was a tango.

Twisting his neck to look back at her, Pete said, "I think I'm feeling it. I'm starting to. But what about the backhand? My backhand could really use some work."

She didn't exactly smile but her jaw softened and her eyes twinkled as she played along with the conspiracy of touch. Bending lower, her hand still guiding his wrist, she slowly twirled him into a swoop, almost a swoon, a shared coiling. Her torso was draped across him. Her chin was resting on his shoulder. Their knees and thighs were nested.

That's how they were standing when a familiar big car with its high-beams on pulled into the narrow street behind the courts and fitted itself between two signs that said No Overnight Parking.

The engine stayed on after the car was parked. Shafts of ugly brightness from the headlights spilled distorted shadows through the fence and across the court.

Penelope let go of Pete's wrist and lifted herself away from their odd but lovely clinch. He felt her stiffen as she lifted, and his eyes followed hers toward the intruding vehicle. She retrieved her paddle, gracefully stepped over the net, and went back to pretending this was just an ordinary lesson. They were rallying back and forth again when the unmistakable big and hatless man with thick dark hair poured himself from the car and started lumbering toward the bleachers.

A couple of steps before he reached them, he called out, "'Lo, Teach. Fancy seein' you here this time of evenin'."

Penelope said nothing, just gave the big man a brief nod that was utterly devoid of welcome.

With a dismissive tilt of his chin toward Pete, the big man said, "This your boyfriend?"

"We're doing a lesson."

"From the way youse was all wrapped up together, I thought maybe he was your boyfriend."

"We're doing a lesson," she repeated.

"Lesson in somethin'."

She put her hands on her hips, her paddle dangling down against her thigh, and she fixed the big man with an eyes-narrowed, chin-forward look that Pete had never seen from her before. It was defiant. It was feisty. It was Jersey. After all, it's where she'd come from, and though she, like Pete, had managed to get away and largely shed the attitude that life in Jersey required from day to day, the toughness was still there when she needed it. "Look," she said, "if you think you're being funny with this stuff, it isn't working. So why don't you just cut it out?"

The big man seemed less chastened than amused. "Nice," he said. "I like the fightin' spirit. But okay, sorry, no offense. Actually, I was just comin' over to make nice and see if youse would like to play a game or two."

"A game?" said Pete. "No, I don't think I'm ready for that. I've never even touched a paddle before."

"So what? Ya got a very strong partner."

"And you don't seem to have a partner at all," said Penelope. "So, no, sorry, it won't work. Some other time maybe. I'd like to get back to my lesson now."

She turned her eyes toward Pete but the big man didn't let the matter drop.

"So happens," he said, "I do got a partner. Inna car. Nice player. 'Specially when he's high. My boss."

Boss? thought Pete. Not just one thug after Gianni, but a thug with a boss? The news made the wine and oysters feel a bit unsettled in his stomach.

"Loves the game, my boss," the big man rambled on. "Can't get enough. He's jonesin' to play."

Pete said, "Why not just hit the two of you? There's plenty other courts."

"I wasn't talkin' to you, rookie. He'd really like to play wit' Teach here."

"Well, it isn't happening right now," said Penelope. "Like I said, maybe some other time."

"He'll be very disappointed," said the big man.

She responded to that with a shrug and softly hit a ball toward Pete. Pete volleyed it back.

"He don't deal well wit' disappointment," said the big man.

Without breaking the rhythm of the rally she said, "Well, maybe that's something he should work on."

The big man crossed his arms and said in a rather whiny, mock-scolding tone. "Now, is that nice? Is that helpful? After he's come all this way down here to see ya?"

"What?" said Penelope.

A ball went right past her and skittered toward the fence. Her immaculate posture crumpled a bit. The lovely arc between her neck and shoulders lost some of its lift.

"You heard me, Teach. Fresh outa the can, and he's come all this way, and you won't even—"

"I don't want to see him," she said. "Not now. Not ever. He damn well knows that."

"Maybe he forgot. Five years away, people forget a lotta things."

"Well, I don't," said Penelope. "I wish I did, but I don't." She turned toward Pete with furious and hunted eyes. "Sorry, lesson's over. I really need to get out of here."

The big man glowered at them as they left the court but didn't try to stop them. Penelope couldn't quite hide her trembling as she climbed onto her bike.

19.

It was a silent ride back to Penelope's small cottage.

But things got noisy as soon as her low front door was opened. A Rat Pack playlist was pouring from the stereo. Frank Sinatra. Dean Martin. Sammy Davis, Jr. Water was running in the sink. An espresso maker was hissing on the stove.

Uncle Gianni had managed to get out of the armchair and was sitting at the miniature kitchen table, his blue-wrapped cast propped on a stool, the dregs of a glass of wine in front of him. Gertie was doing dishes, her hips not quite level against the counter, and attempting in a rather tipsy alto to sing along with "You Make Me Feel So Young." The place smelled of olive oil and flavored bread crumbs and tomato paste.

Gertie stopped singing but kept on washing dishes. "So how was the lesson?"

Pete looked at Penelope. Penelope looked at Pete. Since the lesson itself had been more or less obliterated by what came after, neither could quite find anything to say.

Gertie answered her own question with another. "He's a natural, isn't he?"

Quietly trying to regain her composure, Penelope just nodded.

Pete changed the subject. "How was dinner?"

"Ask Gianni," said his mother, with a quick proud giggle followed by a hiccup. "He's the guest of honor."

"Delicious," the injured man said dutifully, and rubbed his stomach.

"Eggplant parma-john," she announced to the room while drying her hands on a borrowed apron. "Used to be Peter's favorite."

Pete had no idea where this recollection came from. It had never been his favorite. He found it slimy.

"Oh, and Peter," his mother went on, "I hope you don't mind. I grabbed a couple bottles of wine."

"A couple?"

"Well, in case the first one was bad. Then we would've been stuck, right? I mean, they looked pretty old."

A faint dread began droning in Pete's mind. "How old, Mom?"

"Um, really old. I think like 1982. And they had a funny name. O'Brien, something like that."

"Haut-Brion, by any chance?"

"Yeah, that's it. Oh-bree-own."

"Mom, you drank my 1982 Haut-Brion with eggplant parmigiana?"

"Yeah. Went pretty well. Nice and smooth."

"Two bottles?"

She blushed, though this seemed less from embarrassment than being rather pleased with herself. "Well, a glass or two while I was preparing, then a glass or two while we were eating, then a glass or two while we were talking, and it just went. Such a homey evening. Guess we should have saved you some. We didn't."

Pete drew in a long slow breath. This was his mother, after

all. She'd given him life. She'd fed him at her breast. She'd changed his diapers and put Band-Aids on his boo-boos and sat with him through nights of childhood fever. But his last two irreplaceable bottles of '82 Haut-Brion? Paired with slimy eggplant parmigiana, no less? This was pushing it.

"Mom," he said, "I've been saving those bottles for decades. Saving them for something really special."

Looking slightly wounded, and maybe realizing through her tipsy state that she had goofed, she went on the attack. "What, this isn't special enough for you? The four of us here together, healthy mostly, enjoying one another's company. To you this isn't special?"

"I didn't say that. I just—"

"To him it isn't special," she complained to Penelope and Gianni, nestling deeper into her hurt feelings. "Okay, what can I say? My only child. I come to see him, manage to have a little fun mixed in with all the stress and trouble, and for him it isn't special. It's special to me. What would be special to him? The birth of his own first child maybe? Then he'd know what it's like. Not that he's likely to give me a grandchild anytime soon. Not at the rate he's going."

"Mom, how the hell did we get to my giving you or not giving you a grandchild? We're talking about two bottles of wine."

"Exactly."

"Exactly what?" said Pete.

"Exactly, how can you even compare them?"

"Who's comparing them? I'm not comparing them."

"Two measly bottles of wine compared to the blessing of a grandchild. How can you even—"

"Mom, I'm not comparing them, okay?"

"Oh, it's all right, Peter. We all say thoughtless things

sometimes, things we don't really mean. Forget that you compared them. Doesn't matter. Let's move on. So, you did great at pickleball?"

A long half-hour later, Pete was easing his tipsy mother into a taxi that had pulled into the narrow lane. Inside the cottage, Penelope had helped Uncle Gianni get settled in the bedroom and was making up the sofa where she herself would sleep.

Crouching slightly to get back in through the low door, Pete let some breath whistle through his teeth and said, "Sure would be nice to have a little Haut-Brion left over for a nightcap."

"Guess it would," she said. "Honestly, though, I don't feel like anything. I'm just awfully tired, Pete."

She plumped a couple of pillows. He shuffled his feet and looked down at the floor. Finally he said, "Penelope. About what happened. At the courts..."

She glanced sideways at the closed door to the bedroom, then back at Pete from under knitted brows, and said softly, "I don't think I'm ready to talk about it. Not right now. Especially not here."

Pete pressed his lips together and wondered what a real detective would say to that. Speaking in a raspy whisper, he said, "Look, if I'm supposed to help your uncle—"

"Then eventually you'll need to know. I get it. Just not right now."

He kept quiet and tried not to sulk.

After a moment she said, "Probably everybody has their secrets, right?"

"Everybody I've been meeting lately."

"And it's a weird thing, keeping a secret for so long. I mean, it's painful. It's something you're ashamed of, right, or why would you keep it secret in the first place? But then in some crazy way the secret becomes a part of you, some kind of sick treasure even, and you just don't want to give it up. Like you'd miss the guilt if it was gone. It's like, I don't know, like having an ugly pair of shoes that pinch your feet every time you put them on but for some crazy reason you just can't bring yourself to throw them out. That make sense to you at all?"

"Um, well, sort of, maybe."

"Well, whether it makes sense or not, it's sort of what I'm wrestling with. I just need a little time. Can you be patient with me? Please?"

He didn't know what he should say, so he just said, "Sure." And she kissed him on the cheek.

The kiss happened so fast that he wasn't quite certain it had happened at all. Had her lips really brushed against his skin, or was it only a near-miss that left behind an arc of warmth and the sweet burn of a blush?

Either way, he carried the feel of it with him though the low door and back out to the street. Sweeping away the glistening moisture that settled on bicycles and cars during balmy Key West nights, he climbed up onto his pedals but he did not head home.

20.

"I hope it wasn't too late to call."

"Nah, fuck's the difference?" said Bert the Shirt. "I don't sleep good anyway. Nice to be out inna night air. Dog likes it, too, once I get 'im outa bed and get his sweater on."

The sweater in question was cashmere in a bold Argyle pattern of burgundy, yellow, and gray. Bert wore one to match, creating the odd impression that dog and master must have wandered into a fog bank on a Scottish golf course and somehow emerged in the American tropics. Bert and Pete were sitting on the seawall directly across the A1A from the Paradiso; the public restrooms and showers were a few yards to their left, the line of now-closed food trucks stretched away to their right. The dog was hanging out below them, digging up the trucked-in sand of Smathers Beach. It pawed around until it got sand up its nose, then it came out with a spasmodic sneeze that wracked it from head to tail, then it cast a puzzled look up at its master as if to say what the heck just happened? Then it went back to digging until it sneezed again.

"So," the old man went on, "to what do I owe the pleasure of your visit? Havin' trouble wit' your client the stripper?"

"He's not my client," said Pete. "He's just a guy I'm trying to help out. And doing a crap job of it so far."

"Sounds kinda like a client to me, 'cept wit'out ya get paid."

"Whatever. And he'd rather not be known as the stripper. That was a long time ago. He's trying to keep it a secret from my mother and his niece. Afraid they'll get the wrong idea."

"Wrong idea? What's the wrong idea? Guy took his clothes off or he didn't."

"Well, he asked me to keep it quiet so I'm respecting that."

"Very discreet. Very professional. But inna meantime, I gather or you might say surmise that you haven't solved his problem for him or otherwise fixed things up so that his worries are over and he can now live his life in peace and tranquility, amen."

Pete shook his head and looked down at the dog, with whom he felt a sudden kinship. All that digging and getting nowhere. "Not only have I not solved it, I'm not even sure any more whose problem it really is."

Bert said, "Come again on that?"

"Well, it's complicated."

"I had a funny hunch it might be. So what's up?"

Pete shifted a few inches on the seawall and took in a good deep suck of ocean air. It smelled of half-dried seaweed and empty seashells that held just the faintest memory of their former inhabitants, and had an iodine tang that left a pleasant sting at the very top of his nose. "Shit," he said, "where do I even start? Okay. So Gianni has a niece who teaches pickleball."

"The freakin' beautiful one who wears the lime-green shorts and little yellow tops? Who when she isn't teachin' is always out joggin' on the promenade or doin' headstands or those, whaddyacallit, Palooties exercises on the beach?"

"Christ, Bert, you don't miss a trick."

"Try not to. I mean, I may be old as dirt, but I'm still a guy, and I happen to admire female beauty, or I think pulchritude is the fancy name for it, in all its many wondrous variations of color, shape, and size, and I ain't ashamed t'admit it even though I hear you're not supposed to do that anymore, which, excuse me, is just not realistic and goes against nature and is therefore bogus. But anyway, you were sayin'…"

"Right. She's Gianni's niece. They're very close. Apparently he helped her through a very sketchy situation once, but I don't know the details. Anyway, now that Gianni's the one in trouble, she really wants to help. So last night she noticed that the guy who's stalking Gianni, or at least the guy who Gianni thinks is stalking him, has been parking his car over by the pickleball courts, maybe sleeping in it, and has balls that light up at night."

"His balls light up at night? Pete, we talkin', whaddyacallit, figurative here?"

"No, literal. Pickleballs. For playing at night. So Penelope—that's her name—took a wild guess that maybe the stalker has a pickleball partner who doesn't want to be seen during the daytime, so he parks there and they play at night. So she thought it would be a good idea to give me some lessons so that maybe sometime I could get on a court with them and get some information and figure out who the hell they are. You with me so far?"

"I think so, yeah. The lit-up balls thing threw me for a sec, but I think I'm back on track."

"Okay, so earlier this evening, Penelope and I went out for dinner."

"You sly dog. You took her on a date?"

"It wasn't a date. We did it so Gianni and my mother could be alone."

"Very selfless of ya. But it sure sounds like a date to me. Where'd ya go?"

"What's the difference where we went?"

"Just curious. I like to know where people eat."

"Raoul's"

"Ah. Kind of a romantic place. Dependin' onna company, of course. Wha'd y'eat?"

"What's it matter what we ate?"

"I just like to know what people had. People go to restaurants, you're not curious what they had? Come on, ya hear this alla time. One guys says he went to a restaurant, the next guy says, 'Yeah? Wha'd ya have?' I mean, it's natural curiosity. 'Wha'd ya have? Was it good?' I mean, everybody wants to know what the guy at the next table's havin', right? Askin' the waitress, tryin' not to stare at the plates as they go by…"

"Okay, okay. Oysters."

"Ah, I shoulda figured. First date. Oysters. Ya think they're, whaddyacallit, aphrodoozhiacs, or ya think that's just bullshit?"

"I really don't know, Bert. But can we please get to the part that matters?"

The old man seemed just slightly put out by the comment but gave his Argyle sweater a brief tug and rallied quickly. "Well, okay, sure, if you're in that much of a hurry. And if you're sure ya know which part is gonna matter. I mean, it ain't always obvious till after which part a somethin' is the important part. But okay, let's cut to the chase. So you've had your oysters and now you're out onna court playin' pickleball wit' your girlfriend—"

"She's not my girlfriend."

"'Scuse me. You're out onna court wit' a beautiful woman wit' whom you've just been sharin' oysters and no doubt some wine to wash 'em down, and lookin' into each other's eyes, 'cause where the hell else ya gonna look, and then what happens?"

"So she's showing me the right way to hit a forehand."

"Showin' you, like, demonstratin'?"

"Well, no. More like…like walking me though it."

"Sorry, I can't quite picture that. So the two a yas are walkin'?"

"No, Bert. She's holding my wrist and standing behind me and showing me how to swing."

"Like, wit' her arms around ya?"

"Yes."

"Swingin' together?"

"Yes."

"Shweet."

"And then we did the backhand."

"Nice."

"And then the big black car with the creep inside pulled up."

"Bummer."

"Big time. So this big nasty guy gets out, the one who doesn't wear a hat—"

"Which, 'scuse the interruption," Bert put in, "is like a perfect example or you might say illustration a what I was just sayin' about how the hell do ya know from the start what's gonna be the important part a somethin'? Guy doesn't wear a hat. So what? Small detail. Then it gets to be the thing you know him by. Thanks for makin' my point for me. So anyway, this prick shows up—"

"And he walks over toward the court. Very pushy, very sarcastic. Calls Penelope Teach. Me, he basically ignores except to ask her if I'm her boyfriend."

"Ah, so at least I ain't the only one to reach the obvious conclusion that any idiot could see where this so-called lesson is headed if everybody lives long enough for the thing to run it's natural course."

Pete let that pass and just lightly kicked his heels against the concrete of the seawall. "Anyway, then the guy starts sounding sort of pseudo-friendly and says he's just hoping to get a doubles game together. I beg off, since I've never played before. Penelope's looking for an out, so she says it's too bad the big guy doesn't have a partner. And that's when it get weird."

"I'm listenin'," said Bert as he slowly reached down to scoop up the dog and began to stroke its sandy head between the ears.

"Well, it turns out the big guy does have a partner. In the car. Waiting. And, from a few things that get said, it sounds like he's a guy who just finished five years in prison and very much wants to see Penelope, except Penelope never wants to see him again and is very freaked out that he's suddenly showed up."

"Christ, Pete, this sounds like the important part. Why'n't ya tell me this part sooner?"

"You wouldn't let me. You wanted to talk about the menu."

"Okay, okay, fuhgeddaboudit. So this mystery guy inna car, he have a name?"

Pete shrugged and raised his hands, palms upward. "The big guy just said it was his boss."

"Boss," said Bert, stroking the dog in his lap. "This I don't like. The word has, whaddyacallit, connotations. I mean, I don't think we're talkin' about his manager in a mainstream corporate settin', if ya catch my drift. Any idea what the guy was inna hoosegow for?"

"None."

"Ya get a look at him at all?"

"No. He stayed in the car, behind the high beams."

The old man scratched the dog. The dog ran a wobbly circuit

around the old man's crotch then seemed suddenly to be asleep. "So let's think where we're at," Bert said. "Logical, like. Gianni's bein' stalked by the big guy, let's call him No-Hat. But why? Ya figured that much out, at least?"

"No, I haven't," Pete admitted. "That's the question I started with, and I've gotten exactly nowhere. Could be a money thing with the restaurant, though Gianni says everything is square on that. Could be a silent partner trying to muscle Gianni out of the business now that his protector's dead."

"Protector? This I didn't know about."

"A guy named Paulie. From Mulberry Street."

"Ah, probably Paulie Moretti. Kind of a small-time guy. Had some influence, though."

"Well, he was the guy who first set Gianni up in the restaurant. Probably the main owner all along. Died a few months ago. Just before the trouble started."

"So who took over from Paulie?"

"Gianni doesn't know. Everything goes through a middle-man, a guy named Mort who won't tell him anything and might be a liar anyway. He's from Paramus."

Bert stroked the sleeping dog. "Paramus. This I don't like. So we got a money angle, which Gianni thinks it isn't. We got a silent partner angle, but we don't know who the partner is. This means we got bupkis."

"Agreed. Except for one more possibility that seems too crazy to be true."

"Y'ever read the papers, Pete? Nuthin's too crazy to be true."

"Well, okay, then try this one on. Gianni's strip club turned out to be a big hit with gay men. That's why Paulie shut it down. A few of the macho types made a stink, said it reflected badly on their manliness. So badly that there might still be a grudge about it, a grudge that was simmering right up until Paulie died."

Bert shook his head. "Fuckin' troglodytes. Then again, I've heard of equally assholic things. So let's not rule it out. But net-net, I'd still say we got zilch on Gianni's problem. So I think we need to look at the whole thing from a different angle."

"What different angle? Look, Gianni says—"

"Let's leave Gianni onna side a minute. Sorry, but I think we gotta scope out how your girlfriend figures in."

Pete gave a start that almost cost him his balance on the narrow seawall. "But—"

"Look, you're the one who said you're not even sure about whose problem all this really is, so I think we gotta take a good hard look at all the possibilities."

The old man paused from stroking the dog and gave his friend a paternal pat on the knee. "I know it ain't easy," he went on. "There's a complicatin' element a physical attraction and possibly growin' or even mushroomin' or, what's that other word, blossomin' or burgeonin' emotional involvement between you two that can cloud a person's judgment or even make things look the way he wants 'em to look 'stead of how they are, which, at the end a the day, can sometimes lead to disappointment and a lousy outcome. So let's try to be whaddyacallit, dispassionate rather than its opposite, i.e., passionate, which seems to be the path you're headed down and which can be a beautiful and rewardin' thing, just not when you're tryin' to be logical. So let's just cogitate a minute."

Pete fidgeted and wrestled with denial. Denial was winning. The old man cogitated for twenty seconds then resumed.

"Okay, so Gianni thinks he's bein' stalked by No-Hat, though he really don't know why. Now it turns out No-Hat has a Boss fresh outa the slammer who's anglin' to see Penelope. Coincidence? These guys just feel like takin' a road trip together down from Jersey? Fact is, we don't know. Maybe Gianni's the target, like we been thinkin' all along, and maybe the Boss wantin' to see Penelope is just a throw-in, a sentimental journey, like. But maybe Penelope's the one bein' stalked, and maybe trackin' down Uncle Gianni was just a way to find her. Or maybe they're both bein' stalked for different reasons. Tell me why any a those scenarios don't wash."

Pete kicked his heels and gestured with his hands but couldn't find an answer.

"Look," said Bert, "it's hard. I unnerstand. You're gettin' to care about this woman. You'd hate to think she's the one that has a problem or is maybe the reason for Gianni's problem, especially since problems don't usually cause themselves, which prob'ly means there's somethin' she doesn't wanna talk to you about and you don't wanna hear. It's not easy. But inna meantime, if ya want my advice—"

The flummoxed detective leaned forward to receive the old man's counsel, but Bert broke off suddenly before the advice had been given because he just then noticed two ragged men walking toward them down the promenade. They were carrying a windscreen.

21.

"Pineapple, zat you?" said Bert, as the two ragged men were skirting a cone of light thrown by the lamps that fringed the public showers.

The taller of the two men glanced over through the dimness. His glance was not exactly furtive, just extremely cautious. He hated every kind of trouble, and it seemed to him that trouble sometimes started just from being noticed somewhere, almost anywhere. If someone knew his name and called it out, that sometimes made it even worse. It just seemed like people usually thought he was doing something wrong even when he wasn't. So at first he kept his distance and kept his gaze oblique as he squinted toward the seawall. Then he recognized Bert and more or less relaxed.

It would be a stretch to say that he and Bert were friends, but for years they'd coexisted on a snug and tiny swath of land hemmed in by the ocean, bordered on one side by the public facilities where Pineapple did his washing up, and on the other by the food trucks where Bert got his Sno-Cones or occasional slice of pizza, and the two of them had now and then ended up on the same patch of beach to watch the sun go down, and of course they'd spoken, because Bert talked to everyone, including people like Piney who tended to be leery of being talked to.

But now the tall man sidled over, lugging his end of the windscreen and tugging his stockier companion behind, and said hello.

Bert glanced at the rolled-up bolt of fabric. So did Pete. They both pretended they didn't see it, that it wasn't there.

"Nice night for a stroll," Bert said.

Pineapple agreed, then recalled his manners. "You remember Fred."

"Sure I do," the old man said, although he didn't. "How ya doin', Fred? This here's my buddy Pete."

Everybody said hello to everybody. The sound of a wailing siren came up from Duval Street. A Harley revved on the Boulevard. Everyone continued to pretend that the windscreen did not exist. This was more difficult for Fred and Piney, as the thick roll got heavier the longer they stood still with it. The sleeping dog in Bert's lap finally woke up and started sniffing at the fabric. Everyone tried to ignore what the dog was doing.

Fred said, "Well, I guess we'd best be getting along."

Bert said, "Okay, sure. Good seein' you guys."

He waited until the ragged men had nodded their goodbyes and started to move off, then added offhandedly, "Headin' down to Higgs, by any chance?"

Piney looked at Fred. Fred looked at Piney. They resettled their burden in the crooks of their arms while pretending it was non-existent and therefore weightless. Piney hated to lie so he just kept quiet. Fred hated to leave even the most veiled of challenges unanswered, so he said, "And what of it if we are?"

Bert said, "There's a big mean bastard hangin' out down there. Just thought you oughta know."

Fred could not resist saying, "We do know, thanks. That's why we're goin'."

"Ah," said Bert. "Lookin' for a fight?"

"No," Piney answered quickly. But once he'd come out with that first syllable he felt an obligation to go on, to explain. This put him in a no-win situation. Lying would have given him a feeling like biting into something rotten, and he didn't have an acceptable fib on tap anyway. But he also knew that Fred would probably be annoyed with him if he just came right out and spilled the beans. He sought some middle ground by telling the truth but saying it so softly that it could barely be heard above the faint hiss and rattle of ocean foam slipping down through pebbles. "Um, we're just going down there to put this back."

He briefly glanced down at the bundle in his arms, thereby giving it reality.

Fred shot him a disapproving look and spoke to one in particular as though answering an accusation. "Yeah, I borrowed it, okay? For a project I was doin'. Project's over, we're givin' it back. What's the big deal?"

Bert stroked his dog and said mildly, "Who said it's a big deal? Not a big deal to me. You, Pete?"

Pete just shrugged and shook his head.

"Looks heavy though," the old man continued. "Maybe you'd like to put it down a minute."

Fred and Piney consulted with their eyes then lay the windscreen down athwart the seawall. It immediately folded double, as if the fabric itself were in a deep fatigue. The ragged men shook out their arms.

Amiably, Bert said, "You don't mind my askin', what kinda project were ya doin', Fred? I'm curious about all that do-it-yourselfer stuff."

Suspicious of the question but also flattered to be asked, Fred tentatively dialed back his reflex of secrecy and feistiness. "Tried to make a sailboat. Dinghy. Broomstick. Never sailed worth shit. Tried it three, four times. Fiddled with it. Finally gave up."

"Well, good for you for tryin'. I respect a guy that tries."

Fred wasn't used to getting compliments and for just a moment he wavered between fending this one off or pulling it into himself the way a cactus sucks in rain. After an uncertain beat he allowed himself to believe the kind words could be trusted, and they made him briefly generous in turn. "Tell ya the truth," he said, "I got so goddamn frustrated with the stupid boat that I wasn't even gonna bother bringin' back the windscreen. It could've rotted in the mangroves for all I care. But then Piney here went all Jiminy Cricket on me and started saying how it wasn't right and someone could get hurt, but I was all ticked off and didn't wanna hear about it. So Piney went off on his own to do the right thing. And what does he get for his troubles? He gets called a lotta nasty names, punched in the gut, and kicked out of a public park where's he got every right to be. Is that bullshit, or what?"

"Total bullshit," Bert agreed.

Pete finally spoke up, turning his attention to Pineapple. "The guy who hit you. Big thick guy without a hat?"

Piney said, "Never really saw him. He shined a light in my eyes. Sure hit like a big guy, though."

"Total bullshit," muttered Fred, "and I won't stand for it. That's why we're goin' back the two of us. Guy gives us any shit, I go low, Piney goes high, we take 'im down and see whose park it is."

"Or maybe he won't be there," Piney said hopefully. "I don't need to get even, Fred. I just wanna have this over with."

"Yeah? Well, gettin' even is part of gettin' somethin' over with. Christ, Piney, if everybody just took this la-di-da, just walk away kinda attitude, grudges would never get settled."

"Well, maybe there'd be fewer of 'em to begin with. Ever think of it that way, Fred?"

Apparently Fred hadn't. He frowned, turned his face away, and spat over the seawall.

Bert said, "Well, I'm sure you guys'll work it out and handle it however ya think best but, not like it's any a my business, I got a question for ya. If this big bastard's still hangin' around, what makes ya think he'd be alone? I mean, he was there to play pickleball, right? Guys don't do that by themselves. What if there are two big bastards? What if it's a doubles game? Doin' the math, that would make it four. Wit' due respect, Fred, the time-honored I-go-low-you-go-high approach, which certainly has its time and place and a decent track record a felicitous results—could ya really see it workin' against more than one mean bastard at a time?"

Fred said nothing for a moment but his face revealed the fleeting heartbreak of realizing that a cherished plan was flawed. Hoping to salvage it, he said to Piney, "The guy was alone last time, right?"

"Well, I think he was," the tall man said. "But only at the start. By the time I left, he was playing with somebody. I saw the balls flying back and forth. They were lighted up inside."

"Shit," said Fred, and spat over the seawall again.

Bert scratched the dog between the ears and adjusted the tiny Argyle sweater that had gotten bunched up between its pairs of paws. After a moment, he said, "Well, not t'interfere wit' you guys doin' what ya gotta do, but since it looks like your original approach is not quite provin' satisfactory, I'm wonderin' if ya might be open to the possibility of handlin' the situation a little different. A partnership, like."

"Partnership?" said Pineapple.

"Ya see," said Bert, "it so happens that me and Pete are also havin' a problem wit' this guy."

"Oh yeah? What kinda problem?" Fred demanded.

"Well, for one thing, he's been hasslin' a young lady that Pete here is practically engaged to—"

"Now wait a second, Bert—"

"Okay, okay, slight exaggeration for effect. A lady-friend of Pete's. Anyway, someone who it ain't right hasslin'. And on top a that, he broke the leg of a friend of ours."

"Well, not exactly," Pete put in. "He might have caused an accident where someone got hurt. Not a broken leg. Torn Achilles."

"The guy the ambulance came for?" Pineapple asked.

"Right," said Pete. "Happened on court six."

The two ragged men could not avoid a quick and guilty glance at the windscreen. Piney's face was somber. Fred's showed a flicker of remorse before his feistiness kicked in again. "You a cop?" he said to Pete. "You sound a little like a cop."

"I'm not a cop. I'm...I'm a..." Pete was having the damnedest time getting the word out. It was stuck halfway down his throat like an unchewed wad of steak. Finally, on the third try, he said, "I'm a detective."

"Ah," said Fred. "So whatcha been detectin'?"

Pete blushed, and the hot bloom on his neck and forehead reminded him how cool and humid the night had become. "Actually, very little."

"Guys," said Bert, "what ya gotta unnerstand is that this an extremely complex and whaddyacallit, delicate situation, full a possible hazards and dead ends and—whadda'ya call those things that show up afterwards?—ramifications. Right, ramifications. But we'll get it sorted out. We're workin' on it."

We? thought Pete. Well, okay, welcome aboard.

"But inna meantime," the old man went on, "I have to believe that sometime inna foreseeable future, which is a phrase I never really got, since no one ever foresees the future even when it's just, like, twenty minutes up the road...but anyway, I have to believe that sometime soon there's gonna come a time when all the pussyfootin' around and investigatin' will be behind us, and we'll know however much we're gonna know, and things will come to a head, or a boil, or the head of a boil, however ya wanna put it, and prob'ly, since this is how it usually goes, there'll prob'ly be a dicey big-ass confrontation, and if there's one thing I've learned about big-ass confrontations from the ones I been in and survived, it's that it's better to have more guys on your side than the other side has. So what I'm proposin', or askin' as a favor really, is that you guys postpone your very admirable errand until such time that it makes sense for all of us to go down there together and do what we gotta do to get these nasty fuckers out of our lives."

The rambling statement left a bit of a vacuum and a whoosh behind it, like the headlong passing of an eighteen-wheeler, and it was a few seconds before anybody spoke. Then Fred said, "So you want us to lug the fucking thing home again?"

Bert petted the dog. "I know it's a pain, but—"

"But it's the right thing to do," said Piney, who was already crouching down to pick up his end of the well-traveled windscreen. "We're in, Bert. Just keep us posted. You know where to find us. We're still up by the airport."

22.

Pete swiveled his legs and eased down from the seawall, then swept the night-time condensation from his bike seat and headed home.

His bike was not equipped with a rear-view mirror. If it had been, he might have noticed that a large dark car had fallen in behind him as he rounded the curve just past the Higgs Beach courts, and that it continued following at a distance of one block until he reached his house, at which point it veered off unseen as he was locking up the bicycle in the side yard.

He walked up the creaky porch steps and through the unlocked door into his living room, then tiptoed to the guest bedroom and put his ear against the door. His mother, after drinking, with slimy eggplant parmigiana, the two best bottles from his modest and never-to-be-replenished collection of 1982 Bordeaux, was snoring more lustily and fitfully than usual, with brief honks and rising trills interspersed amidst the more general sawing.

He sighed and went to the music room, where he poured himself a jumbo Cognac and put on some Brahms. The music was dark and tangled and tormented and it usually cheered him up, as other people's anguish often does when regarded at a safe remove.

But that night it didn't work. He was too tangled up in worries of his own, too tangled up in other people's secrets. There were things he needed to find out and at the same time dreaded knowing. Especially about Penelope. She seemed so solid, so sensible, so…good. What could she have had to do with these thugs and bullies, with this so-called Boss fresh out of prison? Even just wondering about it made him feel uneasy and vaguely unclean, as if there was something unavoidably leering and salacious about prying into other people's darker sides, their shadowed nooks and crannies, even if you were only doing it to help, and even, or maybe especially, if you feared what you might find there.

He eventually gave up on the music after admitting to himself that he hadn't really been listening anyway. He sat in silence for a while, then poured himself another Cognac and went to bed.

By the time he got up in the morning, Gertie, in her pink robe and fuzzy slippers, had already staked out her strategic position in the middle of the kitchen, perched at the counter between the fridge and stove. She was drinking black coffee and dipping triangles of toast into a bowl of soft-boiled eggs. She asked her son if he had slept well, then frowned down at her breakfast and said, "I really despise soft-boiled eggs. I read somewhere they're good for a hangover. You think that's true?"

"Nothing's good for a hangover," Pete said, maneuvering around her so he could reach the coffee pot.

She poked at the eggs. "With a lot of salt they're not too bad."

He said nothing, just maneuvered around her in the opposite direction and handed her a salt shaker.

"Except I'm not supposed to have a lot of salt. Hardly any. I retain water."

"That's fascinating, Mom."

"I get puffy. Around the eyes. Ankles."

Her son drank his coffee.

"You're very quiet this morning, Peter."

"Sorry, I have a lot on my mind."

She put down a triangle of toast and looked uncharacteristically sheepish for a moment. "I hope I didn't embarrass you last night."

"Oh, don't be silly, Mom. You could never embarrass me."

She picked up the toast again. "Do I detect your usual note of sarcasm in that last remark?"

He tilted his head and drank his coffee.

Her sheepishness vanished as she answered her own question. "Yes, I definitely did." She turned her eyes up toward the ceiling and spoke as though addressing someone on the roof. "I try to be nice, I try to apologize even, and what do I get? Sarcasm he gives me. First thing in the morning, already with the sarcasm."

"Okay, it was a tad facetious," he admitted. "Sorry."

She pouted at her eggs but quickly got over her snit. "It's just that I was having such a wonderful time. Cooking for Gianni in that sweet little cottage. Having you close by. Seeing how nice you and Penelope look together."

"We're not together. She gave me a pickleball lesson."

"Like it would be so terrible if you were together?"

"Don't start, Mom. Please."

"Mister wild-and-crazy bachelor, sitting naked in the hot tub. What, together is a dirty word?"

"Did I ever say that, Mom? I don't think I ever said that."

"It happens to be a beautiful word."

"Who's arguing?" He maneuvered clockwise around her to refill his coffee cup, then retraced his steps and maneuvered counter-clockwise to grab a stale muffin from the fridge.

"Beautiful," she said again.

He took two bites of the muffin, kissed his mother on the cheek, and went off to find Penelope, the woman he was not together with.

23.

Her early clinic was winding down by the time he reached the courts. There were eight students but the nasty man who didn't wear a hat was not among them. The courtside space between the two No Parking signs was vacant. The air was warming moment by moment as the morning shed some of its humid shimmer. The day's first breeze was beginning to stir, putting well-fed bellies in the windscreens and distorting shots over on court six.

Pete left his bike near Penelope's, their handlebars and wire baskets leaning in perfect parallel. He took a seat in the bleachers and watched the aspiring players hack their way through a last few points, have a last few laughs, receive some final bits of advice. When play had finished and people were packing up their gear, Penelope swapped chit-chat with a few of her regulars. Her lips were smiling and her athlete's posture maintained its stoic crispness, but as Pete approached, he could see, even beneath the visor and behind the sunglasses, that her violet eyes were drawn and troubled. Very softly, he said, "We need to talk."

"Not here," she whispered, her lips barely moving and her eyes sweeping the bleachers full of students and acquaintances.

"The pier?"

She offered a small nod and they headed for their bikes.

White Street Pier was just a short ride away, at the end of the sandy path that looped all through Higgs Beach, past the gazebo where no one was allowed to sleep but people racked out anyway, past the empty volleyball court with its patched and drooping net, past the old brick tower that had morphed into a garden club and a refuge for the blue-haired ladies. The pier poked out a quarter-mile

139

into the Atlantic and was really sort of ugly, built of brown concrete, but what it lacked in charm it made up in durability. Hurricane winds couldn't budge it. Storm surges washed over it like bathwater.

Here and there, people were fishing from its edges, catching spider crabs and not much else. People jogged, biked, skated, sped past on electric scooters. Pete and Penelope eased along until they reached the huge but faded compass rose that was painted on the ground at the far end of the pier. They picked a corner where they would not be splashed by the wavelets that slapped against the windward side and arced up in random sprinkles, and sat down on a railing.

Pete looked down at his hands, swallowed painfully through a dry throat, and fumbled for a way to start the conversation. "So, um, how's Uncle Gianni?"

"Doing better day by day. How's your Mom?"

"Hungover. Impossible." He managed something like a smile then said, "Penelope—"

"Yeah, I know. There's a lot I haven't told you, and it's making everything harder and more complicated, and I'm really, really sorry."

"Look, I'm not blaming—"

"I know you aren't, Pete. I'm blaming myself." She swept off her sunglasses, put them on again, and dropped her voice so low that the words barely carried against the light breeze and occasional slaps of water. "It's what recovering junkies tend to do."

Pete wrapped his hands hard around the railing and craned a little forward. He opened his mouth but no words came out.

"You heard right," she told him. "Been clean just over five years now, but there isn't a day I don't remember there's an addict hiding in my skin. That's why I panicked when Duke—that's his name, the guy hiding in the car—showed up last night."

"Your dealer?"

"Ex-dealer. Ex-boyfriend. Ex-guide to the joys of opiates. The guy who helped me almost wreck my life."

"And you've been in touch? You've talked?"

"No way. Not since the night of my last dose."

"But he knew you were living down here in Key West."

"Looks like he found out. I have no idea when or how."

Pete said, "Probably through the guy who's been stalking Uncle Gianni, right? I mean, it ties in somehow, right?"

"Duke ties in with everything. The bastard."

"Do you want to tell me about him?"

She looked off at the horizon for a moment and managed a quick and rueful laugh. "I can try. I mean, I just blew my chances with you—"

"No you didn't."

"—and you're the first guy I've let myself like in a long, long time. Maybe the rest of the story won't be quite as hard."

Pelicans were diving in the shallows. Gulls wheeled and cackled overhead. Penelope coaxed her visor down a fraction to give her violet eyes a place to hide.

"I met him around seven years ago," she said. "At Uncle Gianni's restaurant. I was working there part-time, sometimes waiting tables, sometimes hostessing. I wasn't good at either job. Gianni was just being nice to me, helping me make a little money, giving me a place to go instead of sitting home with my very strict and very bitter Mom. And I just liked hanging out with Gianni. Guess I missed my father more than I admitted at the time. Anyway, I was also taking some college classes, but the truth is I wasn't interested in anything.

Just treading water, basically.

"Sometimes I hung out at the restaurant even when I didn't have a shift, and I picked up a little education about how things really worked. Uncle Gianni was the boss, but then again not really. People were sent to him and he had to hire them. Purveyors' reps showed up, and those were the people he had to buy from. Duke was one of the reps. The company he worked for did the fancy provisions, the veal chops and such. He always showed up in a nice car and a beautiful dark blue suit, and his tie was always a little bit askew. This wasn't by accident. He did it to look cool, and it worked. On me at least. He had this super-confident manner that intrigued me. With Uncle Gianni, he tried to be very pals-y, like they were peers, equals, even though Duke was a lot younger, but there was something sort of smirky about his tone that Gianni didn't like but I sort of did. Childish, of course.

"Anyway, Duke would kid around and flirt with me whenever he came in, as I'm sure he did with every young woman at every restaurant he worked with, and Uncle Gianni noticed, of course, and one day, even though he hardly ever tried to tell me what to do, he told me to keep away from Duke, he was trouble. 'That car,' he said. 'Those suits. They don't come from selling veal. You be very careful with that guy.' Best advice ever, but of course it just made me more curious.

"Eventually, on a day when Gianni was busy with another salesman and Duke and I had a few minutes alone, he asked me out. The way he did it—well, it was halfway between an invitation and a dare. He already knew that Gianni disapproved of him—he had great paranoid radar for that kind of thing—so he knew that if I said yes I'd be defying my uncle and basically sneaking around, and would have to lie or at least not tell the truth about where I went and what I did, and the fact that I'd lied and he knew it would give him a certain kind of power over me, which is exactly how he operated. With everyone. About everything. Always looking for secrets that would give him leverage.

"Anyway, we started going out. Part of me knew from the very beginning that it was a bad idea. So why'd I do it? I've asked myself a thousand times. Stick it to Mom? Get even for my parents' breakup, like that piece of bad luck gave me a free pass to misbehave? Maybe I had a self-destructive streak all along but never noticed it before. Or maybe it was way simpler than that. Maybe I just had a crush on Duke and thought it would be fun to date him.

"And it was fun for awhile. Nice restaurants. Nice hotel rooms where I never quite stayed the night. We had three or four nice evenings before the pills came out. Then one night he pulled a vial out of his suit jacket pocket and poured some tablets on to a night table. 'Percocet,' he said. 'Want some?'

"He was very casual about it, so casual that it was hard to feel shocked or even very surprised. It was like he was offering M&Ms or after-dinner mints or something. I'd never taken hard drugs before. Drank a little bit, of course. Had tried weed, didn't like it much. Stronger stuff, never. So I said no, I didn't want it.

"He gave a smirky little shrug, said, 'Okay,' and started to sweep the pills back into the vial. But then he seemed to change his mind and left them sitting there on the night table. They'd fallen into a pattern sort of like a dragon's tail. I had a hard time pulling my eyes away from them. He asked me, 'Why not?'

"I said, 'I don't know why not. I just don't. I don't need it.'

"He picked up a couple of pills, washed them down with something from a flask he'd brought along. Then he said, 'How do you know you don't need it? People don't know what they need till they've had a taste of how much better they could feel. Pain gone, worry gone. Nothing left but calm.'

"He leaned back against a pillow and closed his eyes. I tried to stop looking at the pills. Eyes still closed, he said, 'You're scared.' It was a statement, not a question. There was a kind of creepy gentleness, a devilish patience, mixed in with the taunting.

"'Afraid,' he went on, 'you'll end up under a bridge somewhere with all your worldly goods in a rusty shopping cart. You know what's wrong with you, Penelope? You believe what you read in the paper, those scary stories about users going down the tubes. And let's be real, some do. The weaklings, the ones who'd be a mess, drugs or no drugs. But you know what you don't read in the papers? You don't read about the smart users whose lives are going just fine. More than fine—tremendous. Why? Because they go through life relaxed. Knowing they have the world's best reward to look forward to at the end of the day or the end of the week or whatever. Lemme show you something, Penelope.'

"And with that," she went on, "he opened up the robe he was wearing and showed me his tracks. I'd never noticed them before. They were on the inside of his leg and very faint. 'You see?' he said. 'One shot every four, five days. Not more than that. Discipline, Penelope. That's all it takes. Discipline and a little bit of brains and you can have a brief trip to paradise anytime you like.' He paused, then very slowly started sweeping the Percocets back into the bottle. 'But hey, if you're not interested…'

"Well, I took one, of course.

"Duke smiled. 'That's the way,' he said. 'Start small. Start light. Just a pill or two.'"

She broke off for a moment, stared at Pete, then looked out across the water. A couple of jet-skis slammed by. An osprey circled overhead, its wings making only the tiniest adjustments as it rode the currents. She took her visor off, then, with a sort of quiet fury, ran a hand through her short black hair before putting it back in place. "Are you sure you're okay hearing this?" she asked. "I know it isn't pretty."

"And I know it's in the past," he said. "Go on."

She took a deep breath and let it out slowly. "Well, it didn't take me long to get hooked. Guess I was one of the weaklings. Two weeks, a month, I don't even remember. The cravings got to be too much. It was still just pills at that point, but I was in Duke's control. He stopped being quite so nice to me. He had me—why bother being nice? He took me on his rounds a few times. Driving his fancy car around, selling meat to restaurants, then stopping at a nearby park or alley to deliver dope to kids. He even made me carry the bags a couple times. I think he did it just to get me nervous so I'd need a fix.

"Understand, I was still kidding myself that I could hide what I was up to, that I could pass for clean and carry on. I was still doing my shifts at the restaurant, still trying to be on time and more or less on top of things, still trying not to let down Uncle Gianni. And Duke got nastier and nastier about that. If I told him I had to get to work, he'd take it as an opportunity to talk about how Uncle Gianni wasn't quite the great guy I thought he was, and there were some things he knew that would bring him down to size, and all this obnoxious stuff that he just wouldn't let go of. I think I started hating Duke for that. I think he knew I hated him. Probably he wanted me to. I mean, it all got pretty twisted.

"And then it got even more twisted. One day I told Duke I needed some pills. He said he didn't have them. That was bullshit. He had plenty. But he wanted to get me shooting up. 'Why not go straight to the source?' he said, in that smirky voice of his. 'Why not go for the mother lode?' So he taught me to shoot heroin. I'd hated needles my whole life. Hated them to the point of fainting. Now I couldn't wait for the next one. Between shots, nothing quite seemed real. I started missing shifts at work, telling tangled lies I couldn't even remember I'd told. I was slipping fast but I had just enough sanity left to be disgusted with myself. Then one day I got caught. Did I do it on purpose? Was it your basic cry for help? Or was I just too messed up to be careful any more? I don't even know.

"Anyway, I shot up in the ladies room at the restaurant. Not the first time I'd done it. But this time I took a little bit too much. I must've nodded out. I don't know how much time went by. I heard someone knocking on the door. It sounded very far away. I heard Uncle Gianni call my name. I tried to answer. Voice wouldn't work. Maybe I whimpered. Gianni broke the door down, jerked the needle out of my arm, and brought me to the hospital. Once I was out of danger, he got down to the business of having Duke taken care of."

"He went to the police?" Pete asked.

"No. No way. He went to Paulie. The Mafia has rules, after

all. Selling drugs is a no-no. Guys do it all the time, of course, and bosses look the other way. But when a guy starts pushing heroin on a young woman who happens to be a member of the family, that crosses the line. So Paulie ordered a beating for Duke. Apparently it was quite a thorough beating. Face cut, elbow broken, many teeth knocked out. A lot of pain. And what does a junkie do when he's in pain? Takes more junk. A lot more junk. So Duke, who was so proud of his discipline and self-control, finally overdid it. He got caught one night passed out in his nice car with about a hundred thousand dollars worth of product in the trunk. So he went off to prison and I went off to rehab."

"And it worked," said Pete. "The rehab, I mean."

"Eventually," she said. "It was hell at first, but why linger on it? What finally turned things around was meeting a hard-ass counselor whose approach was finding a good addiction to fill in for the bad addiction."

"Good addiction?" said Pete.

"Exercise. Do it hard enough for long enough and you'll get the dopamine and the endorphins without the drugs. So that's what I do. Get a craving, run five miles. Still feel like a hit, go grind in the gym till I'm lightheaded or play pickleball till the blisters come. That's what's been holding me together, Pete. That, and being really careful not to make another dumb mistake with a guy who turns out to be rotten."

She paused, shrugged, tried to smile but it didn't quite work. Her eyes slid away and downward as she tried to meet Pete's gaze. After soldiering through her unsparing confession, her voice turned oddly shy. "So there it is," she said. "I'm an exercise addict with a screwed-up past and a terrible fear of getting close to someone, and if you don't want anything more to do with me, I get it. I just hope you'll see this through for Gianni. His troubles are all my fault."

"Maybe they are and maybe they aren't," said Pete. "I won't give up until we know. But either way, I wish you'd stop blaming yourself."

She said nothing, just looked out across the water. A long moment passed. She was sitting very still with her hands on her knees but she couldn't quite keep from fidgeting. With fingers that were not quite steady either, Pete reached out to touch her. His fingertips had barely grazed hers when she pulled her hands away. There was both panic and sorrow in her face. "Pete…that's very kind. I guess I'd love it if you held my hands, but I just can't do it. Not yet. I'm sorry. Please don't be angry with me. It's really better if I just ride and run a few more miles."

He was still perched on the railing as she bolted down, climbed onto her bike, and pedaled fiercely down the pier.

24.

"Who is it?" Gertie sang out from the guest room when the knock came at the front door. Thanks to the coffee and the hated runny eggs, she'd wrestled her hangover to a stalemate and was thinking that a slow swim and some stretching in the pool might get her back to feeling herself. So she had shrugged off the pink bathrobe and was just about to get into the floral pattern bathing suit with the modest ruffled skirt.

"Key West Flower Shop," answered a gruff voice trying not to sound like one.

"What?"

"Florist, lady. Flowers."

"Oh, how nice! Just a moment, please." She put the bathing suit aside and pulled the pink robe on again. As she stepped into the fuzzy slippers, she was thinking Oh, that Gianni. So romantic. Thanking me for the eggplant parmigiana. Thinking of it even with his leg in a cast and all his other troubles. Such a gentleman!...Or wait—is it even possible they're from Peter? It's not my birthday. It isn't Mother's Day. His way of apologizing for being sarcastic with me, maybe? Stranger things have happened...

As she always did with deliveries, she briefly checked her hair and lipstick before limping to the door. Excited, curious, she reached for the doorknob and pulled it open. Standing in front of her was a big man who was trying hard to smile. He didn't have a hat on. Teasingly, he seemed to be holding the bouquet behind his back. She tried to peek around him but his torso was too wide. "Is there a card?" she asked. "I hope there's a card."

"No card," he said, as he grabbed her arm, swiveled her around, and stuck the muzzle of a .38 between her shoulder blades. "No card, no flowers, no noise. Not a peep. Just walk, old lady. We're goin' to the car."

He half pushed, half carried her down the porch steps and over the humped sidewalk where the traveler palm had lifted up the pavement, then he bundled her into the back seat of the dark sedan and slid in beside her. As the car pulled away from the curb, she primly rearranged the panels of her robe and said, "Look, I don't know who the hell you think you are, but you can't do this to me. You won't get away with it. My son—"

"I've met your son," snarled the hatless man. "He's a wuss."

"A wuss? Oh, really? You think he's a wuss? You stay tuned, buster. You'll find out who's a wuss. And what the hell are you, a hero? Kidnapping a woman with a hip replacement in her bathrobe? What does that make you? A chicken, that's what it makes you. A big lousy chicken. With a gun, no less. Grabbing a lady in a bathrobe. For this he needs a gun?"

The man behind the wheel said, "Tell her to shut up."

He told her. She didn't.

"And which one of you big chickens is the guy who put my Gianni in the hospital and broke his leg? Why? Why'd you do that? Gianni never did anything to you."

The driver said, "You're wrong on that, old lady. He did."

"What? Wha'd he do that you're making all this trouble for him?"

Instead of answering, the man behind the wheel reached into a leather satchel at his side, plucked out a pill, and swallowed it. No water, just the pill. Gertie studied him in the rear-view mirror. He had thick curly hair, a square jaw, and might have been nice-looking except for the squashed nose, a long scar that ran from the edge of his right eye all the way down to his chin, and a mouthful of bad dental work that made his teeth look too big for his gums.

"So wha'd he do?" she asked again.

Again there was no answer. By the time the car had wheeled onto U.S.1 and barreled past the marina into unfamiliar territory, the old woman had used up her spurt of feistiness and indignation and was just beginning to notice that she was terribly afraid.

"Where are you taking me?" she asked.

The two big men didn't answer that one either.

♨ ♨ ♨

"I don't know about this partner business," Fred was saying.

Pineapple didn't answer right away because he was too absorbed in raking the patch of ground around the hot dog wagon that was their home. He was using a bamboo rake that Fred had borrowed from a landscaping job some years before, and he loved everything about the process. The soft but crisply clattering sound the rake made when it was dragged against the mix of sandy soil and small stones. The way some of the raked stones hopped up between the tines like they'd been tickled. He loved the way the fallen mangrove leaves got bundled up and rolled almost like they'd been swept up in the surf. Most of all, he loved the way the ground looked when he was finished. Leaves gone, bigger stones removed, the earth lightly rippled with trenches as regular and delicate as corduroy.

"I mean," Fred went on, "why should we throw in with them? We don't know what their deal is. Maybe it's something really serious. Maybe it'll bring in the cops. Hell, they've already had a guy carted off in an ambulance."

"We said we'd help."

"You said we'd help."

151

Piney lifted the rake and cleared a few broken leaves that had been spiked by the tips of the tines. "Okay, I volunteered us. I admit it. But I said it for both of us and you didn't say anything and now we gotta do what we said we'd do."

"It's just gettin' so frickin' complicated. First, you were gonna put the stupid windscreen back. That's one guy. Then you and me were gonna do it together. Two guys. Now it's us and Bert and that detective who don't detect nothin', plus at least two big bastards on the other side, maybe more. Who knows? I'm losin' count, and I just don't like how complicated it's gettin'."

Speaking as softly as the rake had whispered, Piney said, "Well, no offense, Fred, but there wouldn't be any complications if you didn't steal it to begin with."

"That part wasn't complicated. Grabbing the goddamn thing was easy as pie. It's puttin' it back that's become a royal pain in the ass. And besides, I didn't steal it. I took it. Stealing is when you take something away from somebody that owns it. This was just hangin' there. It didn't belong to nobody."

"Fred, it's County. It's a park. It belongs to everybody."

"Yeah, yeah, yeah. But have y'ever noticed that everybody is a lot like nobody? What are you, some kinda fuckin' Communist?"

"I don't know. I've never really thought about it. Ya have no money, what's the difference?"

"Well, do yourself a favor and don't start thinkin' about it now, 'cause if you start thinkin' about it and decide you are one, then one of is movin' out, 'cause I don't see myself bein' roommates wit' a Communist. So let's quit it already wit' arguin' politics 'cause where the hell's it get ya anyway, and okay, I'll go along wit' whatever Bert asks us to do, but I'm tellin' you right now that this will be the last and final time I will lug that fucking thing up and down the promenade. Fair enough?"

"Sure," said Piney. "Whatever."

He went back to his raking, leaving the ground lightly rippled in perfect parallels.

25.

Pete sat on the railing at the end of the pier for a few minutes after Penelope had ridden off. When she was telling him her story, he really hadn't known what he should say. Now that he was sitting there alone, he didn't even know what he should think. Except maybe that people, when you really got gut-deep, were fated to be strangers to each other. Secrets sometimes got revealed but, even after the seeming climax of the revelation, mysteries still remained. Penelope had been a junkie. But why? The when and how could be described and maybe even understood, but the final why of it could only be guessed at or mock-explained with tired catchwords.

But maybe the final why of it wasn't the part that mattered most. What mattered most was that she'd stopped the skid and saved herself, and done it mainly on her own. She hadn't sought a rescuer, hadn't bought into some white-knight fantasy; in fact, once she'd launched into her solitary redemption mission, she seemed to have run like hell from any man who might imagine himself a savior but could just as likely turn out to be a tempter who'd mess her up again.

Reflecting on her vigilant aloneness, Pete finally got past what he was supposed to be thinking and broke through to what he was actually feeling, which was tenderness and admiration mingled with a slightly guilty relief. How often did he come across a beautiful woman who was even more of a commitment-phobe than he was? A shared terror of involvement might have been an odd basis for a possible bond between two people—but then again, weren't all relationships a little bit odd, especially in the beginning, before their oddness had become a habit and therefore passed for normal?

He eased down from the railing and headed home, though he was in no great hurry to deal with Gertie and her hangover and her discombobulating mix of compliments and zingers. So he took a meandering route past Southernmost Point with its lined-up tourists all waiting to take the same bad photo of their sunburned faces shadowed by their hat-brims; and through the gentrifying jumble of Bahama Village where fussily restored cottages in lavender and peach stood next to shacks with plywood windows; through the tidy pastel falsity of Truman Annex whose new arrivals mistakenly imagined that wearing linen shorts would make them look like locals; across the part of Duval Street that smelled like margaritas at any hour of the day or night; through the above-ground cemetery with its mordant epitaphs and family crypts suggesting file cabinets; and finally to his own house, from which he did not immediately realize that his mother had been kidnapped.

The front door was unlocked. But then, it usually was. No problem. The living room looked the way it always did. He stepped inside and, trying his best not to sound preoccupied or grumpy or, God forbid, sarcastic, called out, "Hi, Mom."

Getting no answer, he moved quietly to the guest room door to see if Gertie had perhaps gone back to sleep. But her door was open, the bed had been made, and her floral pattern bathing suit lay where it had been tossed on top of the light quilt.

He took a quick glance at the kitchen, but she wasn't there, so that meant she must be sitting out by the pool. Except she wasn't.

He called out to her again, this time in a louder voice, in case, say, she was puttering in the side yard. When no answer came, he began to be concerned. Not worried. Not yet. Just concerned.

He went back to the kitchen and surveyed it more closely, scanning the corners of the countertops, the nooks beneath the cabinets, the places where she would probably have left a note if she'd gone out. But there didn't seem to be a note. Possibly she'd sent a text that he didn't hear come in. He checked his phone. There was no text.

Concern had now ratcheted up to worry. Not yet dread or panic. Just worry.

He called Uncle Gianni and asked too quickly, with none of the standard niceties, if Gertie happened to be over there. Apparently he did a lousy job of masking his anxiety, because Gianni immediately said, "No. Is something wrong?"

Not knowing if something was wrong or not, Pete ignored the question and asked if Gianni and his Mom had spoken on the phone.

"No, not today yet. Everything okay?"

Trying not to spread his fear around, Pete said, "Yeah, yeah, everything's fine. But please, if you hear from my Mom, have her call me right away."

He hung up the phone and started pacing, lurching, randomly blundering through the house and yard, looking everywhere with a spreading, gnawing expectation that whatever he found would not be good. Might she have taken a fall in the shower? Would he find her unconscious and bleeding in the tub? But everything was fine in the guest bathroom, her array of pill bottles arranged neatly on a shelf, her battalion of cosmetics on another. Had she passed out while gardening in the side yard, doing more than she should have in the unaccustomed heat? Would he find her crumpled under a bougainvillea, garden-gloves still on, a trowel stuck in the ground where she'd fainted? No, the side yard was empty. Baffled, sliding toward blind panic, his search careening beyond the rational to the desperate, he raced to the backyard and lifted the lid of the hot tub, as though she'd somehow slipped in and closed the cover over herself. There was nothing in the hot tub except a tiny dead and bloated lizard.

Finally it occurred to him to check the wicker basket that hung from a nail on the porch and served him as a mailbox. Flushed, breathing heavily, he barged out through the front door that he'd entered by so calmly only minutes before, and that was when he found the note. It was scrawled in pencil on a torn-off piece of paper about half the size of an index card. The handwriting was unsteady, some letters crabbed and some spread out. The words ran together without punctuation. Pete held the note by the very edge and read it.

He blinked and swallowed and read it again. Then he lowered his arm and shook the paper as if maybe he could make the writing fall off and disappear.

It didn't disappear, so he read it a third time and then did the only thing he could think of in that moment. He called up Bert the Shirt.

26.

Bert was lunching on conch fritters down at Ducky's on Duval when the call came in from Pete, so the old man cut short the conversation and just asked his friend to join him. The jangle and the forced high spirits of Duval Street were the last things Pete needed just then, but that's where Bert was, so he went.

The old man offered him a fritter before he'd even quite reached the table on the deck above the sidewalk or had time to say a word.

Pete just shook his head.

"Ain't quite as good as they useta be. Less conch, more breadcrumbs. Waya the world, right?"

"Bert—"

"Ya think it's any different wit' veal cutlets? Same deal. When's the last time ya had a really good veal cutlet? Less meat, more crumbs. Either that, or the meat tastes like a shoe 'cause it ain't real veal. I dunno what these places stick in there, but veal it's not."

"Bert, um—"

"Sure ya don't want a fritter? Half a fritter? If not, I'm givin' it to the dog."

Pete shook his head again. He'd managed by now to perch on the edge of a chair. Bert bent down to feed a crumble of fritter to the chihuahua at his feet. Pete took advantage of the brief silence to blurt out, "Those bastards grabbed my mother!"

The old man straightened up again, quickly by his standards. "They what?"

"They kidnapped her. They came to the house when I was out and took her."

Bert considered that a moment, then said, "Your mother's just been kidnapped and you let me go on and on about veal cutlets?"

"I didn't let you. You just did."

"Jesus. Sorry."

"They left a note," Pete said.

He coaxed it carefully from the pocket of his khaki shorts and handed it over. Bert held it out at arm's length. Then he pulled it in so close it almost touched his nose. Then he tried a few intermediate positions. He looked like he was playing a trombone. Finally he said, "I can't read the fucking thing wit'out my glasses. What's it say?"

Pete didn't need to take the scrap of paper back. He had the message memorized by then. "It says 'trade you the old lady for an hour with penelope courts at midnight bring gianni.'"

Bert reached down, lifted Nacho onto his lap, and stroked the dog's head like he was stroking his own chin. He pursed his heavy lips, gave a contemplative tug to the placket of his red silk shirt with the yellow monogram, and said, "Had lunch yet?"

"I can't eat, Bert. How could I eat?"

"Nah, I figured ya couldn't. How 'bout a drink, though?"

Without waiting for an answer, he signaled the server with an elegantly minimal lift of his chin. He ordered a glass of wine for Pete and an Old-Fashioned for himself.

"Situations like this," he resumed, "main thing is stay calm."

"Stay calm? Bert, it's my mother."

"Which makes it that much more challengin' to maintain one's equilibrium or also equanimity, which is basically sayin' the same thing two different ways. This much I grant you. But it wouldn't help nothin' losin' our composure. So one thing at a time. Any idea where they took her? Where she is right now?"

Pete shook his head and to his complete surprise he suddenly choked up. Not knowing where his mother was; the deep and simple fact of it gave him a desolate and empty feeling, an ancient terror, like being a kid lost in an endless glaring supermarket. He knew where he wished his mother was. Back in Jersey. A thousand miles away. But safe. Somewhere he could call her on the phone, even if mostly what they did was argue. But someplace known, somewhere he could find her. Maybe even visit.

Bert stroked the dog and gave his friend a moment to collect himself. Then he said, "Okay, ya don't know where they took her, that's prob'ly a good thing."

"How? How the hell's that good?"

"'Cause if ya knew, it'd be human nature to go runnin' there, maybe force the issue, storm the Bastille, so to speak, and that makes people jumpy, and that's when bad things tend to happen. This way, ya can go slow, think it through. The guys who grabbed her—we know anything more about 'em than we did a day ago?"

"Yeah, a lot," said Pete, as the drinks were being delivered.

He and Bert clinked glasses, then the old man took a few seconds to fish the maraschino cherry out of his cocktail and dangle it above the dog. Its back paws firmly planted on its master's scrotum, the chihuahua shot up like a barracuda striking at a shiny lure and nipped the alcoholic fruit right off the stem.

"For one thing," the younger man went on, "we know that the boss guy's name is Duke, that he used to sell provisions to Gianni's restaurant, and that before he went to prison he was Penelope's boyfriend and also her heroin dealer."

Bert stopped midway through his first sip. "Run that last part by me again?"

"You heard it right. Penelope's been in recovery five years or so. I don't think she'd mind my telling you. It ties in with the whole mess."

"She's okay now?"

"She's great. She needs a fix, she pulls her sneakers on, runs five miles, and makes herself even more beautiful."

"And this Duke guy. Just a dealer? Or a dealer and a user?"

"Both. That's how he got caught. Overdid it on the pain management after a Mafia beating for selling dope to family members. Nodded out with a carful of opioids."

"Gianni was in on the beating?" Bert asked.

"I don't think so. Not personally. He told Paulie Moretti the shit that Duke was doing. Paulie took care of the rest."

Bert massaged the dog and sipped his drink. Pete glanced off at the procession of slightly desperate merrymakers cruising up and down Duval. Harleys groaning under beefy guys in denim and chains. Bachelorettes already plastered and wobbling by on ankle-breaking shoes. Hairy men in sundresses. Purple-haired women in studs and leather. The occasional shy couple strolling past with eyes averted, secretly wondering if maybe they should have picked Orlando.

"So if this Duke was a junkie when he went inta the joint," Bert said, "he's prob'ly a worse junkie now. Ya got money inna joint, ya get all the junk ya want. Passes the time, I guess. But I don't like it that we're dealin' wit' a junkie, 'cause that means ya don't know who the hell you're dealin' wit'. Jekyll and Hyde, these guys."

Pete didn't like the sound of that at all. When he reached for his wineglass, his hand was trembling a bit. He tried to make it stop by clenching his teeth. That only made his jaw ache. He wanted to ask Bert if he thought the thugs would hurt his mother but he was afraid he'd start blubbering if he asked the question and neither Bert nor anybody else would know the answer anyway.

"But here's the part I still don't get," the old man went on. "Who is this Duke guy really mad at? Gianni's the one's been gettin' hassled. But now it's Penelope he wants to trade your mother for. But he also wants Gianni there at midnight. Why? Let's say all he wants is payback for the beating he took however many years ago. Why not just beat up Gianni? If all he wants is to get a hold a Penelope, why does Gianni need to be there? If what he really wants is to round 'em up and kill 'em both, there's less complicated ways to do it. So what's up wit' all the frills and doodads? What the hell else does he want?"

Pete said, "I have no idea. He's a junkie, right? Who knows how his mind works?"

Bert said, "Well, fucked-up people have fucked-up logic, but that don't mean it ain't logical in a fucked-up sorta way. Wha' did Penelope and Gianni say about the situation?"

"The situation?"

"The note. Your mother gettin' grabbed."

"I haven't told them yet. I wanted to talk to you first."

Bert stroked the dog with one hand and adjusted his own shirt collar with the other. "Well, that's very flatterin' and all, but seein' as how the two of them are sorta the guests of honor and I'm just kinda the outsider here, and especially since Penelope is supposed to be the grand prize in the prisoner exchange, I think it's only right and fittin' that we should talk to them asap."

"We?"

"Well, look Pete, if ya'd rather I didn't come hornin' in I wouldn't be insulted, but what we got here is a sketchy situation where people could get hurt and it happens to be the kinda thing wit' which I got a small degree a familiarity and in fact is kinda in my wheelhouse, false modesty aside, and if ya think I might possibly be of help inna strategy or armaments department, I'm offerin', but then again if you want me to keep my big nose out of it, all ya gotta do is say thanks, old man, no thanks, go home. So it's really up to you."

Without waiting for an answer, he gestured for the check.

27.

The long-abandoned shrimp depot on Stock Island had been rented on the cheap and with no questions asked and it turned out to be the perfect place to stash a hostage for a day or so. The wide metal door on the water side of the badly leaning building had been rusted shut for years. The only way in or out was through a narrow side door that was easily locked and bolted. There were no windows. Bare light bulbs glared here and there like stars that had just about died. Inside the cavernous space, voices took on the irritating resonance of untuned bells or cheap speakers with a short; but no sound escaped through the steel skin of the warehouse, or if it did, it was soon lost amid the roar of dredgers and the seismic pounding of pile-drivers setting up piers for the luxury marinas that were moving in where the commercial fishermen used to dock.

Still, the depot did retain at least one feature of its colorful past: the stink. It was a multi-layered stink that traced the devolution of a shrimp from its admired status as a briny, meaty morsel to its reeking decline into a gray ammoniac mush of ooze and shell. Mingled with decaying seafood was the funk of long-departed workers who sweated the particular kind of tropical sweat that streamed down inside the heavy rubber aprons that were meant to keep the slime and shrimp guts off their street clothes. It was a smell that had seeped into the concrete floor and could not be scrubbed or bleached away.

It was the first thing Gertie noticed when No-Hat pushed her through the narrow side door. "P.U.!" she said, "how the hell you expect anybody to breathe in here?"

The big man shrugged. "Breathe, don't breathe, I don't give a fuck."

She breathed. Like everything else in life, the stink was something a person could get used to if she had to.

She took a moment to look around the mostly empty warehouse. There weren't any chairs, but a few ancient sorting tables still stood here and there. She limped over to one and tested its surface with a fingertip. It seemed to have been lacquered over with petrified slime and was slightly sticky, but not too. She put her backside against the table's edge and tried to hoist herself up onto it, but with her balky hip she couldn't quite manage. She tried again, got no closer, then called out to her captors, who were leaning against the far wall, vaping. "Can one of you please help me up," she said. "I can't stand all day on this bum leg."

The two men looked at each other as if deciding whether they should just ignore her altogether. Then Duke put the e-cig in his pocket and walked over to her. His eyes measured the height of the table and the level of her hips. Moving closer, he said, "Okay, lady, we can do this. Lean on me."

She bent her head toward her captor's shoulder and put her arm halfway across his back. He reached behind her and, through the pink robe, cupped his hand under her arm. "Okay," he went on. "One, two, three."

She stretched, he lifted, and she found herself sitting on the table. She primly settled the panels of her robe and said, "Thank you."

To her surprise, he said, "You're welcome."

"The way you did that, it was very kind."

He didn't answer but he didn't walk away.

"It was gentle," she went on. "Made me wonder if maybe you're not as bad a person as you seem to be."

"Too late for wondering, lady. Don't bother."

"It's never too late."

"Oh, Christ. You know how many times I heard that, lady? It happens to be bullshit. Sometimes it is too late. Way too late."

"Well, we just happen to disagree on that. And please don't call me lady. My name's Gertie."

She held out a hand.

He didn't take it. "Gertie, look, I got nothing against you personally, but you're right in the middle of something I have to do, so we're not gonna suddenly be buddies. That just isn't in the cards. Don't try."

"What is it you have to do? Why do you hate my Gianni so much?"

"You've asked me that before, Gertie. And if you keep on asking me, it's gonna make me very angry, and I don't want that to happen. Not right now. I'm saving it for later. When I can use it."

"But why?" she persisted, as he was turning away. "Do you think he cheated you in business? Did he insult you in some way?"

He twisted and glanced back across his shoulder. His face had darkened, making the long scar on his cheek seem to glow a whitish pink like the flesh of just-caught shrimp. "Let it go, lady. Just let it go."

"Maybe he wronged you without knowing it. If he did, he'd apologize. He'd make it up to you. He's a big enough person to do that."

Duke's eyes narrowed, his skin was crawling at the hairline. "Listen, what he did, there's no making up for. The funny part? Maybe it wasn't even his fault, what happened. But something happened and there's no way to fix it. The closest I can get is to destroy him. That's just how it is."

"Kill him? You want to kill my Gianni?"

He kept sidling over toward his leather satchel, then grabbed a pill from it and set it between his lips with unsteady fingers. By the time he'd swallowed it his face had rearranged itself into a forsaken parody of a smile. "Did I say kill? Maybe you haven't been paying your best attention, Gertie. I said destroy. There are other ways of destroying someone, maybe better ways. Like by way of someone he loves."

"Me?"

From across the stinking warehouse, No-Hat suddenly let out a dissonant, percussive, "Ha!"

Duke said, "No, Gertie, not you, though I gotta hand it to you for self-confidence. Kind of impressive, really. But I'm talking about someone he's loved and taken care of for a long time now."

"Penelope? You wouldn't—"

"Oh, but I would. With pleasure. With great pleasure. With Gianni watching. You still think I'm a nice guy, Gertie?"

28.

"Those sons of bitches did what?" said Uncle Gianni, his neck and forehead flushing scarlet and his hurt leg twitching in its blue-wrapped cast.

They were all crammed into the cozy little cottage, four people and a curious chihuahua that kept sniffing everybody's ankles and slinking through the narrow gaps between the close-packed furniture. There wasn't much space left over for air, only for the humidity that put a sheen on skin and a wavering shimmer in the light that slanted through the louvered windows. Terse introductions had been made. Bert and Gianni, friends of friends, understood each other without much need of explanation. Penelope and Bert, locals on a tiny island, already recognized each other and required only names.

Pete said, "They grabbed her in broad daylight. Right from the house." He handed Gianni the note.

Gianni read the brief message. "Cowards," he said. "Chickenshits. If they lay a hand on her—" He left the statement uncompleted and just pressed his lips together. He couldn't even stand except on crutches. No position to be making threats.

His niece reached over and took the scrap of paper from him. She glanced at it and her skin went pallid beneath the wholesome glaze of suntan. "It's all my fault," she said. "I'm so, so sorry."

"It's not your fault," her uncle said.

"It is. That poor sweet Gertie. Going through hell. All because I messed up so bad."

"It's not your fault," her uncle quietly insisted.

A moment passed. The dog's paws ticked against the floor. Bert cleared his throat and said, "'Scuse me, maybe it ain't my place to barge in on a family discussion about whose fault is what and what fault is whose, but I'm wonderin' if maybe it might be more useful and productive if we put aside this very understandably human but maybe not so fruitful approach of blame or self-blame or not-self-blame et cetera, and just bring it down to a question of what's really goin' here so we got a better chance a dealin' wit' it and nobody gets hurt that don't deserve it. Would that be okay wit' everyone?"

The others worked their way through the tangled-up speech and nodded.

"So, Penelope," the old man went on, "this bad guy, this Duke, I understand you previously had a pretty, let's say, complicated relationship wit' 'im."

Pete shot her an apologetic glance. "I felt I had to tell him. I thought he needed to know."

"Sure, I get it, it's fine," she said. "It is what it is. I'm not in hiding. Not anymore." To Bert, she said, "We had your basic toxic fling that lasted a few months. We did hard drugs together for a while. He was my supplier."

"And I gather that it ended badly," Bert said.

She managed something almost like a laugh. "Well, I went to the ER and he went to prison. I guess you could say it ended badly."

Bert picked the dog up from the floor and gave its head a rub. "And even so, even after all that, he's so eager, or desperate is more like it, to see you again that he kidnaps an old lady who happens to be your uncle's girlfriend and maybe your new boyfriend's mother. Why? I mean, wit' due respect, maybe the guy's just still head over heels in love wit' you and who could blame 'im if he is, but kidnappin' old ladies, this is not the way guys in love generally behave or think is gonna get them anywhere. So why else?

I'm just tryin' to figure how the whole thing hangs together."

"It's gotta be my fault," said Uncle Gianni. "I mean, they met at my restaurant. Otherwise she never woulda met that scum. I shoulda done more to keep him away from 'er. It's my fault. Gotta be"

Bert stroked the dog and said, "Please let's not backslide inta that whose-fault-is-what routine."

Pete's eyes had been darting around the room from speaker to speaker and he'd been feeling slightly embarrassed but not surprised at having nothing to contribute. Then he suddenly said, "Wait, I have a question." He looked at Penelope. "Did Duke know you'd moved out of Jersey? Did he know you were living down here?"

"I'm pretty sure not. I did everything I could so that he wouldn't know. Covered my tracks. No forwarding address. No way I wanted to be found."

Sounding almost like a real detective, Pete said, "But Gianni started feeling hassled at the restaurant a few weeks ago. By the big guy without a hat. Isn't that what you told me, Gianni? That you felt like you were being stalked."

"Yeah. That's when it all started. Same guy I saw down here. He was hangin' around at the restaurant, around my car. Then he was onna court when I got hurt."

"So my question," said Pete, "is whether the guy was really stalking you or just hoping that somehow you would lead him to where Penelope was. I mean, Duke knew you two were very close. Sooner or later there'd be a visit. And sure enough they followed you to Key West."

Bert leaned forward, shrunken elbows on knobby knees, and said, "Which brings us back, albeit wit' a slightly deeper understandin', which is always a good thing and a plus, to the naggin' question that we started wit', namely, what's this sick bastard's motive for makin' all this trouble? Is this his loony waya showin' he's still in love wit' Penelope, or is he mad at Gianni, who he knew before the screwed up romance angle even got thrown in? So Gianni, y'ever have any trouble wit' 'im in business?"

"Nah, none at all. You know how it is, Bert. He was told what to sell. I was told what to buy. The money got shuffled back and forth. No problems there."

"Okay, not a finance issue. But if I understand correctly," the old man said, "at some point you complained to your mutual boss about the drug-dealing bullshit, and this guy took a beating."

"Well-deserved," said Gianni. "Thing is, though, I doubt I was the only one complaining. One single complaint, Paulie wouldn'ta come down so hard. Probably woulda been a warning. And a month or so went by between the time I bitched and when the beating happened. So who knows if he ever put two and two together? He mighta. Or might not'a."

"Might or might not'a," echoed Bert. "Okay, so much for that avenue a inquiry."

A puff of breeze moved the light curtains for a moment but died before it could bring any drier air into the cottage. Penelope lifted up her visor and dabbed at the damp skin just below her hairline. "Well, listen," she said, "if we're putting it all out there, trying to figure what makes this guy tick, I thought I should mention this crummy, empty feeling I used to get sometimes. That he was dating me for spite. Not romance. Not love. Not even sex. Spite. Here we've been wondering if he's doing all this insane stuff because he's still in love with me, but what if he never loved me at all? Getting me to fall for him, tempting me with drugs—what if it was all just for spite?"

"But spite for what?" said Bert. "This is what we're tryin' to get to."

Penelope just turned her palms up and shook her head.

Gianni said, "I wish to Christ I knew."

"Well, whatever it is," Penelope said, "I'll be going to him at midnight. Taking Gertie's place. Of course I will. It's my worst fear in the world, being mixed up with him again. I still have nightmares about it. Somehow he gets power over me. He saps my will. He makes me nothing. I fall back to where I was. Sometimes I'm trying to scream but can't make any sound. Sometimes I wake up and I'm gasping. He's a serpent. He's the devil. But I'll go to him and find out if I'm strong enough."

"I won't let that happen," said her Uncle Gianni.

She patted his wrist and gave him a wistful smile as a thank you for the gallant but futile words.

There was a silence. Bert tugged on the chihuahua's ears. Then he said, "Well, I hate ta say it, but I think it's gotta happen."

People dropped each other's gazes at the disappointing statement. Fingers fidgeted. Feet scuffed against the floor. If even Bert the Shirt was giving up, then the situation must be not just dire but hopeless.

"Or at least," he went on, "we gotta make it look like it's happenin'. Go through all the motions. Right up to the last second."

Pete said, "Whose last second, Bert? They have my mother. They'll probably be armed and—"

"And these are serious considerations that need to be seriously considered and which we ain't had time to seriously consider yet 'cause we weren't yet acquainted wit' all the ramifications a the situation, or ya might even say scenario. Now we're more a less clued in, and fortunately we have till midnight to cogitate and strategize and get the lay a the land and scope out the battlefield, so to speak, which is to say we still got time to make a plan which might even turn out to work if we all stay calm and everybody does their part and no one gets too jumpy. So what I'm sayin' is everyone sit tight and try not to get a bellyache from worryin', and me and Pete'll put our heads together and see what we come up wit'. Zat acceptable to everyone?"

Penelope and Gianni nodded. Pete said, "Well, um, sure, Bert, sure."

"Good," the old man said, slapping his hands on his knees to signal the end of the meeting. As he slowly rose from his chair, he cradled the dog and casually asked his detective friend if he happened to own a gun.

29.

The afternoon had mostly slipped away by the time Pete, Bert, and Nacho emerged from the cramped cottage into what seemed an impossibly spacious world of light and air. Without the low ceiling pressing down on them, the sky seemed not just infinitely tall, but as if billowing and burgeoning higher before their very eyes. Unmasked by curtains and louvers, the low sunshine didn't just glow, it throbbed. The flat, straight Key West streets, narrow though they were, appeared to stretch without barriers toward horizons that teased and receded and beckoned onward.

For a couple of blocks, the two men walked in silence, weighed down by the puzzle they were facing. As they went along, the dog sniffed everything and peed selectively on weeds and fenceposts. At some point Pete said rather sheepishly, "Um, Bert, about that gun."

"Yeah?"

"I know I have one, but I'm not sure where I put it. Maybe behind a stack of CDs I haven't listened to in years. The be-bop section, I think."

"No one listens to be-bop anymore. Gives ya a headache. So the gun, I gather y'ain't shot it in a while."

"Long while," Pete admitted.

"It have bullets, this gun?"

"Somewhere. I put 'em in a special place. Behind some books, I think. Hemingway probably."

"Ya still read that guy?"

"Not in years. Does anybody? I figured the bullets would be safe there."

They strolled another block. Nacho went into his familiar crouch and fixed his master with that pleading look. As Bert was gathering the miniature turds he glanced up and said to Pete, "No offense, but I got a question for ya. Have y'ever fired that gun?"

"Oh yeah. Once. When I bought it. Shop had a practice range. This was like fifteen years ago."

"Fifteen years," the old man said as he straightened up and dropped the doo-bag into someone's garbage can. "Well, do me a favor, Pete. If ya find those bullets, don't put 'em in."

"But—"

"It ain't like ridin' a bike, my friend. Things go wrong. Just bring the gun for show. It'll make a nice distraction or whaddyacallit, diversionary thing. Mine'll be loaded. What I'm thinkin', we shouldn't need more than one."

"What you're thinking?"

The old man didn't answer, and in fact he raised a finger to his lips before realizing it was the same hand that had just disposed of the doo-bag, so he quickly lowered it again. But he had acquired many superstitions over the course of his long life—he still picked up a new one now and then, though the old ones never, ever went away—and one of the most fundamental was that it could only bring bad luck to discuss a plan of action until you were pretty sure you had it all thought through, and even then you shouldn't discuss it until you were pretty sure it would work, and even then you shouldn't discuss it because bad luck could still creep in to mess it up and make it seem like it had been a bad plan all along and you'd look like an idiot and wish you'd kept your mouth shut. So he did.

Nothing more was said until they reached Higgs Beach. It

was close to sunset by then and narrow slabs of shimmering cloud—lavender, peach, brick red, parakeet green—were starting to pile up on the horizon like psychedelic pancakes, the way it seems to happen only in Key West. The ocean showed no waves, just a webby blanket of froth. Flat sunshine stretched the shadows of the footprints in the sand, making them appear as mighty dunes.

The pickleball courts were full, players flailing, sneakers squeaking, the syncopated pock of hard-hit shots rising above the background hum of traffic and chatter.

Bert the Shirt noticed none of this. Not the crazy sky, not the twinkling ocean, not the games or the noise they made. He was focused only on surveying the park for its soon-to-be role of battlefield. With Nacho in his arms and Pete straggling mutely at his side, he studied the points of ingress and egress around the fences, the angle of the bleachers, the placement of the streetlights, the clumps of trees that might provide the hiding spots. Finally, after as long a silence as Bert ever allowed himself, he quietly announced, "I think it just might work. But we're gonna need help."

"So, either of you have children?" Gertie asked.

The three of them were having dinner. Hours before, when the stink of the shrimp depot had been vile in their nostrils and the terror of captivity had been a burn in Gertie's spine, eating would have seemed unthinkable. But by now the stink was just the atmosphere they breathed and being a hostage was simply a fact of life. Gertie had even shed most of her self-consciousness about being out in her pink robe and slippers. Just proved that people could get used to anything, and quickly.

No-Hat had run out for Chinese and they were eating out of cardboard containers. Gertie sat on the sorting table and the two men leaned against the metal walls. The food was bad, but people had to eat, and Gertie tried to put it out of her mind that this dried-out chicken with soggy cashews might be her final meal. Even so, how could you have dinner with people and not try, at least, to make a little conversation? So she asked if they had kids.

Duke was eating egg foo yong with a fork. He said, "Don't be ridiculous, Gertie. Bring kids into a screwed-up world like this? No way."

Gertie said, "There are other ways to look at it, you know."

"Yeah, I'm sure there are. I don't need to hear 'em."

No-Hat was having flat noodles. He got to the end of a string of them and suddenly, astonishingly, for a brief interval at least, the snarling thug became a doting father. He said, "I got two."

As if she'd just proved a point, Gertie said, "You see? That's nice. Boys or girls?"

"One of each. Seven and four." He put his container on the concrete floor, wiped his hand on his pants, took out his phone, and went over to show the old lady their pictures. "This is Kyle and this is Rosie."

They were ugly kids but Gertie said they were adorable.

Duke said to No-Hat, "Don't be getting too palsy-walsy, okay? The old broad's our collateral, not your long-lost aunt."

Ignoring that, Gertie said, "You're lucky to have two. Me, I only have the one. Peter."

"Yeah, I met him," No-Hat said. "We didn't exactly hit it off but I guess he seemed okay."

"Multi-talented," claimed Pete's mother. "Straight-A student. Terrific athlete. Captain of the debating team. Charming, clever. Could've done anything in life. I sometimes wonder why he moved all the way down here."

No-Hat said, "Well, I guess ya never know."

Duke said, "Enough with the socializing. Let's not make this any harder than it has to be."

The big man went back to his noodles.

Duke looked at his watch, then at the leather satchel that he always kept quite close to him. He reached into it and grabbed a pill. He'd lost interest in the food by then.

🌴 🌴 🌴

"I don't know," said Fred. "It sounds a little crazy and pretty freakin' dangerous."

"Well, it is," admitted Bert. "Bot'."

The four men and the chihuahua were gathered around a campfire in the mangrove clearing where Fred and Piney lived. The daylight was gone, the dark and waxy leaves having gobbled up the last of it, and Bert and Pete had had to use their cell phone flashlights to find their way past the roots and snags on the skinny pathway that branched off the road. Nacho, on a shortened leash, had made futile lunges at lizards and toads. Fred, skeptical of unannounced visitors, had been ready with a raised machete when they'd first stepped into the clearing. Pineapple had barely looked up from his meticulous arranging of the fire.

"So look," Bert went on, having very gingerly lowered himself down onto a slab of coral rock, "I'm not gonna sit here and bullshit ya that this little gambit is as elegantly conceived and elaborately planned as, say, D-Day, and if you guys can come up wit' a better approach, I'm all ears. But inna meantime, we got a midnight appointment that we gotta keep, and we got two damsels in serious distress. Not one. Two. Two damsels versus a drugged-out desperado who you have no idea what kinda mood he's gonna be in or what the hell he's gonna try to pull. So I'm askin' you to help us rescue 'em. Is it a lot t'ask? Hell yeah. Then again, how often does life give ya the opportunity to do a double-damsel save?"

"We'll do it," said Piney, slightly repositioning a hot coal with a stick. "'Course we'll do it."

"Now wait a second," his friend protested. "Last time we messed around with that screen it was just a big freakin' waste of time."

"This time it won't be," the old man promised. "Might be a fiasco, might be a disaster, but what it won't be is a waste."

"I just wish I knew a little more about what the hell I'm getting into."

"Look," said Pete, swatting at a mosquito that had landed on his neck, "these guys kidnapped my mother. An old lady with a limp. That's how low they are. And they'll exchange her for a beautiful young woman—"

"Your Mom's sure kept her trade-in value," Fred put in.

"—who has a pretty awful history with the bad guy, which, respecting her privacy, we don't need to go into—"

"And who's uncle, by the way," interrupted Bert the Shirt, "is the guy who got hurt on court six the other day, which is really when the whole big shitstorm started, and for which you just might have some small degree a culpability, which is not to say it was entirely your fault but maybe a contributin' factor, which would mean or at least suggest to me that, in addition to the common decency angle to help out people in distress, be they damsels or otherwise, or young or old and wit' a limp, there would also be a moral responsibility and you could even say et'ical imperative to help make right what ya helped go wrong. So, no pressure, but I don't see how youse could sleep tonight knowin' that this tragedy is unfoldin' while the two a youse are safe and snug inside your hot dog. Then again, it's up to you."

"I'm doing it," said Pineapple. "For sure."

"Thank you," said Bert, and twitched the dog a couple of

inches farther back from the popping embers of the fire. "Two guys would be better."

Fred looked away and spit on the ground. "All right," he said, "I'm in."

"Beautiful," said Bert, as he began the gradual and delicate process of rising from his rock. "Be in place and good to go as of 11:30."

30.

"I just feel so goddamn useless," Uncle Gianni said.

"You're not useless," said Penelope. "You're my hero."

"Some hero. Maybe I'll hit him with my crutch."

"You're my hero because you're kind. How's the eggplant?"

It was 9 pm. Penelope had been out for another run, around the cemetery, past the marina, up the promenade to the airport. She'd showered, put on yoga clothes, and reheated last night's parmigiana for her hobbled uncle.

He tasted it, lifted an eyebrow, and managed to shoot his niece a sideways smile. "Well, it's no worse than yesterday."

"It isn't good?" She herself wasn't having any. She nibbled a few melon slices.

"Compared to what? Ya know, restaurant food, what makes it good is fat and salt and no one has to do the dishes. Home cookin', it's all about the attitude. This was made wit' love. She looked proud when she put it onna table. So that makes it terrific. Sort of. Little garlic mighta helped."

He had a couple of bites because it was in front of him. But he didn't really want food and he didn't want chit-chat, he just wanted the time to pass till midnight. He glanced at the clock. It was 9:02.

He couldn't help himself from saying, "I can't believe I let you go out wit' that guy."

"You didn't let me. I sneaked."

"I shoulda been payin' more attention."

"Then what? I would have got around you anyway. And if I didn't, then I would never have known what you were saving me from and I would have been ticked off that you were treating me like a kid. So it had to play the way it played. There wasn't any other way."

"Maybe, maybe not. I mean, does shit just happen or do people let it happen? Who knows? Either way, I'd really like to kill that guy. I'm serious. I'd like to wring his neck. I really would."

"Please don't say that, Uncle Gianni."

"Bad karma?"

"The worst. But look, there's no need. He has no reason to hurt Gertie. It's me he wants to hurt. And I won't let him."

"Very brave, Penelope, but—"

"It doesn't matter what he says to me. It doesn't matter what he does. I will not be hurt. I've decided that. I will not be hurt. I said it over and over while I was running. Whatever happens, I will not be hurt. I'm as sure of it as anyone can be."

🌴 🌴 🌴

Bert was feeding the dog. This was harder than it sounds. The water had to be just the right temperature to soften up the kibble, so Bert always tested it against his wrist. The kibble had to be just the right proportion to the wet food or it didn't look right, so the wet food got added by the teaspoonful. The food bowl had to be placed in just the right position on the mat so it would leave room for the water bowl, then the water bowl had to be refilled and put back without sloshing while Nacho was attacking the food and spinning around and getting underfoot. If all went smoothly, the old man would have to bend down and stand up again four times. If the water got spilled and the floor needed wiping, make it five or six. It was a workout.

While the dog was eating, Bert put up an espresso in his ancient, dented stovetop pot. The dog finished its meal long before the coffee was ready, so the old man gave it a biscotto. While they were both crunching their cookies, they had a little conversation. Bert said, "Gonna tell ya a little secret, Nacho. Just between you and me. I don't know how much much longer I can keep on doin' this crazy stuff. Kinda takes it outa ya. Know what I mean?"

The dog looked up at him with what he took for perfect understanding.

He went to his closet to select their outfits for the night's adventure. It was not an occasion for the flamboyant colors and snazzy accessories he generally favored. What was called for was stealth. He picked matching cashmere sweaters in charcoal gray. Boring but appropriate.

Then he got out the step-stool and tried not to notice the fear in his legs. The step-stool was only three steps high but a goof on any one of them could mean game-over. He clutched the frame as he climbed, then the clothes-pole that stretched across the closet, then the shelf that held the hat-box where he kept his snub-nosed .38. When he reached for the box, the top slipped from his hand and spiraled to the floor. But the gun was nestled in its oiled tissue paper just as he'd left it after the last time it was needed. It felt heavier every time he got it out, but he still knew how to use it.

🌴 🌴 🌴

Pete's house felt very empty in a way it never had before.

He'd lived alone there for many years. It was his choice. It was how he liked it. He didn't want to have to talk to anyone before he'd had his coffee. Indoors or outdoors he went naked much of the time. He liked to put on whatever music he felt like hearing whenever he felt like hearing it, either whispering or blasting according to his mood. He liked deciding when he'd eat or go to sleep or wake up in the morning; or not deciding, just letting it happen with no one else's rhythms to consider. He liked the sounds the house made late at night or when there was a wind shift and the palm fronds scratched or when the rainstorms pounded on the metal roof.

But this evening the house just sounded hollow.

For some minutes he wandered randomly from room to room like someone who had misplaced his cap or car key but forgotten midway through the search what he was looking for. He went to the music room and switched on the amp but was defeated by the chore of choosing music. Upstairs, in his bedroom, he lay down briefly but the mattress seemed somehow to eject him, to scorn the attempt to relax or rest.

He went downstairs again and took some eggs from the fridge. Once he had them in his hands, he realized that he didn't feel like eating them and didn't want to bother cooking them. He put them back in the carton.

And went to the guest bedroom. He'd been dreading going there but he was coming now to understand that his aimless meandering through the house was just a way of getting ready to step into his absent mother's room.

He switched on a light. Her bed was neatly made, her floral bathing suit with the modest skirt lying at the foot where she had tossed it. He peeked into her bathroom, at the shelf of medications and the shelf of make-up and rouge and lipstick and whatever else she used to make peace with her age. The room smelled of her too-sweet perfume and the stuff she used to make her thinning hair look thicker.

He sat down on the edge of her bed. That's all he intended to do; sit there for a minute. But somehow his legs swiveled up and his head lowered down toward the pillow she had slept on, and in what felt like no time at all he had fallen into a peaceful and delicious nap.

31.

The humidity was high and there was a glaze of condensation on Pete's windshield when he went to pick up Bert and Nacho. It was 11:30 and the neighborhood streets were nearly deserted. The tourists were all crammed into a handful of blocks downtown. The locals were mostly in bed. Cats were slinking here and there through shrubbery and under cars. Crickets were tirelessly rasping.

In front of the Paradiso Condominium, Bert eased into the passenger seat and settled the chihuahua in his lap. "Get any rest?" he asked.

"A little. You?"

"Had an espresso. Maybe nodded out a little in fronna television. 'Bout like usual."

When they'd driven a few blocks toward Penelope's small cottage, the old man went on. "You and me, Pete, we're the only ones who know the whole plan."

"You don't plan on telling on Gianni and Penelope?"

"I think it's better not. If they don't know, they can't give a tell. A tell would be bad. A tell would mess up everything. Better we just spring it. Ya got your gun?"

Pete patted a pocket of the light jacket he'd thrown on.

"Don't show it till ya hear the dog," the old man advised. "Not just any dog. This dog. Make sure ya got the sound right." To the chihuahua, he said, "Sing, Nacho."

The dog started singing. The sound it made was not quite a bark, not quite a howl, not quite a yelp. It consisted of three rising notes and was very loud and shrill in the confines of the car. Trying not to wince, Pete said, "Fine, Bert, I got it."

Bert raised a finger and said, "Okay, Nacho, that's enough."

The dog stopped at once. The old man patted its head.

Penelope and Gianni were waiting in their alley. She opened the back door for her uncle and held him up while he maneuvered with his crutches. His extended leg in its blue-wrapped cast took up almost the whole back seat. She squeezed in against the door and they headed to the Higgs Beach courts.

Pete parked on the ocean side of the road. There were lots of empty spaces. The diagonal white lines picked up a dim sparkle from the streetlights and the nearly setting moon. They walked across the pavement, Nacho tugging at his leash, Gianni's crutches making him bob up and down like he was on a carousel. Without exactly deciding to, Pete lightly put a hand on the small of Penelope's back. Without exactly deciding to, she put a hand on his shoulder.

The courts were dark and silent. At the far end of the park, a few homeless people were bedded down on the cushion of soft needles at the base of the casuarina trees. The parking space between the two No Parking signs was as yet unoccupied. The usually boisterous bleachers were empty except for a few abandoned beer cans and tequila bottles, a tattered backpack that someone had left behind, and a lumpy bunch of fabric piled on the topmost row. Bert led the little group to a spot just behind the rickety structure where the streetlights were dim and the metal seats cast slatted shadows.

At five till midnight, the old man peeled off from the others and went to walk Nacho among the leaning palms, black as paper cutouts, beyond the land-side fence. The others stood close enough to feel the heat pulsing from each other's flanks but had nothing left to say. Penelope's breathing was deep and rhythmic. The rubber tips of Gianni's crutches made occasional squeaks against the ground. Pete kept straightening his jacket against the weight of his unloaded gun.

At midnight a big dark car pulled into the snug space between the signs. Two doors clicked open. Three figures emerged. Gertie, in her robe and slippers, limping, her untended hair askew, stood next to No-Hat. Duke slid out from the driver's seat, his leather satchel in his hand. The car doors slammed shut and the three of them moved unhurriedly toward the courts and into the broken shadows of the bleachers.

When they were a few strides away, Pete, not knowing he was about to speak, called out, "Mom," and took a lurching step in her direction.

No-Hat flourished the gun that had been pressed against the old lady's ribs and said, "No closer, sonny boy."

Duke added, "Not till we've had our little chat. Not till we've worked out the terms of our exchange." He put the satchel down at his feet. To Penelope, he said, "And how you doin', baby?"

Her voice sounded very far away. "Fine."

"Clean?"

"Yes."

"Ever think about me?"

"Not if I can help it."

"Good. I don't think about you much either. Thirty, forty times a day maybe. Which is really kinda funny considerin' that at the start I didn't give a shit about you one way or the other. You didn't matter in the least. I hope that hurts your feelin's."

"It doesn't," she said.

"Then I guess I need to try a little harder. You were a pawn, a tool, an instrument. Cute? Yeah, I grant you that. A challenge to get into the sack? Not as much as you might like to think. Tough to get you hooked? Not really. But anyway, it didn't matter. I was never after you. I was out to get your Uncle Gianni."

"Why? But why?" the hurt man asked in a clenched, congested voice. He rocked forward on his crutches, fingers numb from squeezing the handles. "What the hell did I ever do to you?"

"We'll get to that," said Duke. To Penelope, he said, "Your wonderful, perfect, gentlemanly Uncle Gianni. He ever tell ya he used to run a crappy little strip club?"

Gertie, seemingly oblivious to the pressure of the muzzle against her side and not sounding in the least bit scandalized, said, "Really? You used to run a strip club, honey?"

Before Gianni could answer, Duke was going on. "Only it wasn't an ordinary crappy little strip club. Not on Ladies' Night, at least. Was it, Gianni?"

The man on crutches said nothing.

"G'ahead," Duke goaded. "Tell your adoring niece and girlfriend here how you used to prance around in your little leather jockstrap, half-drunk secretaries and Village fags stuffing dollars in the cup."

Gianni looked down at the ground for an instant, then glanced in turn at Penelope and Gertie before staring hard at Duke. "Yeah, okay, I did that. Long time ago. Best option I had. Proud of it? No. Ashamed? Not really. Embarrassed? Yeah, I guess. A little embarrassed. So what of it? You come alla way down here t'embarrass me? You happy now?"

Duke said nothing, just returned the stare.

Gianni went on. "And how the hell you even know about that? You woulda been a kid."

"That's right," Duke said. "A kid. A kid is what I was. So how do I know about it? I know about it 'cause my father used to talk about your act. A lot. Seemed to have some weird kinda thing about it. I'd hear him tellin' my mother late at night. Confessin', like. These weird feelings he was havin.' Couldn't make heads or tails of it. And my mother cryin'. This was a little while before he finally came out. Right around the time he wrecked my family. Wonder if you remember my old man, Gianni. Was a regular for a while. Ran with some buddies from Brooklyn."

Gianni pressed his lips together as his mind riffled through the decades. "Freddy? The guy who was most bent out of shape about the show? Who busted up the place last time he was there? Freddy's your father? And he came out? Well, I say good for him."

"Maybe. Not good for my mother. Not at all. She couldn't handle it. Went to pieces. Fell apart."

Gertie said, "No offense, Duke, but that's her problem, not your father's."

Duke said, "And what are you, the family therapist? Wit' a kid who doesn't wanna live within a thousand miles of ya?"

Pete said, "Hey look, that isn't why—"

"This ain't about you anyway, so just shut up," Duke said. "This is between me and Gianni. Gianni who thinks it's swell that my old man turned out gay. But what about me, Gianni? What about the shit I got inna schoolyard, the laughing and mocking and bullying inna neighborhood?"

"That was ignorance," said Gianni. "Just stupid Brooklyn ignorance."

"Yeah, well you try listenin' to that ignorance day in day out when you're a kid. See how it makes you feel. See if it makes ya hate the father ya used to look up to. See if it makes ya ache for a way outa the pain. Anything, as long as ya can stop feelin' for a while. You try it."

Penelope said, "So it's Gianni's fault your father's gay and that's why you turned out to be a junkie? Come on, Duke, that's the lamest bunch of excuses I ever heard. Your father's gay because he's gay, not because he went to a strip show. And you're a junkie 'cause you just can't stay away from junk. Don't look for someone else to put it on. That's what losers do. Keep thinking like that and you'll never get clean."

"Get clean? Who said I wanted to get clean? In fact, what I feel like right now is getting high. Very high. That's what this little party is about."

Slowly and deliberately, he bent down, grabbed his leather satchel, and placed it at chest height on one of the bleacher benches. All eyes converged on the bag and the world seemed to stop as he reached into it. The breeze died. Palm fronds hung limp. He pulled out a small bottle of water, a bag of white powder, and a big flat-bottomed spoon that he balanced on the seat. With practiced nonchalance, he poured in the liquid, pinched in the heroin, picked up the spoon and heated it with a lighter he pulled from a pocket. When the mixture was cooked, he reached into the satchel again and pulled out a hypodermic.

As he was sucking the dope into the syringe, he said, "Well, whaddya know, silly me, I prepped too much. There's two nice doses here."

He pulled a second needle from his bag, held it in a stripe of light, and wagged it for a moment like a hypnotist's watch. "Anybody wanna join me in a hit? Maybe you, Penelope. With your stripper uncle watching."

"Forget it, Duke. Not now. Not ever."

"A little tempted, maybe?"

"Not tempted enough. Not close."

He filled the second syringe. His hands were no longer quite so steady. His scarred face was taking on a clammy sheen. He said, "Well, that's really a shame, 'cause I don't feel like gettin' high alone. I had enough of that in prison. Now I want some company. Sure I can't persuade you, baby?"

She said nothing, just glared at him.

"A shame," he said again. "Two good doses. One's enough for an excellent high. Two would probably be fatal. But if I can't get some company, I guess I'll just give 'em away." He tossed a sideways glance at Gertie. "Maybe to the old lady. In the neck."

Pete rasped out, "You leave her—"

Duke ignored him and said to his hostage, "Except for the first sting, it would be painless, Gertie. That much I promise. Not a bad death at all. And you would have the comfort of your son right here. And your boyfriend looking on. So I guess that's about it for you, old lady. Unless Penelope can get over herself long enough to take your place and give me just a little bit of satisfaction." To Penelope, he said, "So whaddya say, baby?"

"Duke—" she began.

"No more talk," he said. "No more lectures. Yes or no?"

He gave a nod to No-Hat. The big man tightened his grip on Gertie and tugged back her hair so that her crepey neck was stretched like that of a calf about to be slaughtered. She whimpered once then was silent. Duke, his scarred face now twisted and sickly glistening, shakily held the two needles just below her ears. "Yes or no?"

In the darkness behind the courts, a small dog barked. Three rising notes.

Pete pulled his empty gun from his jacket pocket, drawing the thugs' eyes.

Then a single shot in the air from Bert's old .38 rang out from behind the fence, and by reflex Duke and No-Hat wheeled toward the pop and whine of it. In that distracted instant, Pete lunged at his mother, tackled her, and together they rolled to safety as the lump of fabric suddenly plummeted from the top step of the bleachers. The unfurling material wrapped the killers in black netting, and the weight of Pineapple and Fred, the patient heroes who'd been curled inside, knocked them to the ground and held them pinned until the fight was out of them. No-Hat's futile kicks and punches gradually lost their snap, and by the time Nacho came yapping at the fracas, Duke was lying deathly still beneath the windscreen from court six.

EPILOGUE

"Jeez, that must've been scary," said Pineapple, "having those needles so close to your neck like that. I mean, I was looking straight down through a wrinkle in the windscreen and I could see how close they were. And his hands were shaking pretty bad by then."

"Well, standing there in my robe and slippers after being cooped up in that stinking warehouse all day wasn't exactly a picnic," said Gertie, as she sipped her third glass of Prosecco.

This was happening a few weeks after the midnight confrontation, at a small housewarming party at Gianni's new condo at the Paradiso. His furniture had finally arrived from Singapore, which Bert had by then learned was not a town in China. The cast had been taken off of Gianni's injured heel and he was getting around fairly well in a lace-up boot—well enough to do the cooking. There were sausages with peppers and onions, calzones stuffed with spinach and ricotta, three-color salad festooned with shreds of pecorino. No eggplant, but lots of wine.

"But you know," the old lady went on blithely, "scary as it was, I always trusted that nothing really bad would happen. Because Peter was there. I knew he'd have it figured out."

Pete came close to choking on his Barbera. "Mom, I didn't figure out anything. Bert figured it all out. He did the planning. Fred and Piney did the fighting. Me, I did nothing. All I did was stand there."

"So modest," said his mother. "Never taking credit."

"Actually, you did quite a bit," said Bert, as he fed Nacho a morsel of sausage. "When you pulled the gun, the timing was perfect, so when I fired mine there was just enough confusion that all the rest could happen."

"Big deal," said Pete. "I still have reflexes. Might as well give credit to the dog for barking."

"Which I do," said Bert. "I absolutely do. I mean, let's face it, the bunch of us, we're not exactly a crack corps a hand-picked special ops. We're just regular and kinda random folks who happened to get teamed up, and if we didn't all pull together and reach deep inside to find the moxie to do our job and help each other out, and I include the dog in this, well, someone coulda died."

"Well, someone did," said Fred, who was sitting on an ottoman with a big plate of food on his lap and a wineglass that kept getting empty. He wasn't used to drinking wine and he knocked it back like it was beer. "That Duke guy. The pusher. Ya think he meant to end up with the two needles in his arm or did it just happen in the tussle?"

"He was pretty handy with a needle," said Penelope, who was sitting on a love seat next to Pete. They were noshing from the same plate. They were both in shorts and neither recoiled when their knees happened to rub together. "I think he just wanted his life to be over. Sad really. Just a waste."

Pineapple said, "And the way his buddy, the big guy, just left him laying there and drove off —that wasn't right. Some friend."

"Well, I'm glad he got away," said Gertie. "He has two kids."

"Mom, how you even know that?"

"What, you spend all day with someone and don't see inside of them a little bit? I asked. He showed me pictures."

"That's my Gertie," Gianni said. "Nice to everybody."

"Wonder how things turned out for that Freddy guy," mulled Bert. "I mean, comin' out at that time, in that neighborhood, wit' those kinda friends, and especially after actin' like a loudmouth hater all that time before, that musta took a lotta guts. I hope things turned out okay for him."

"Well, things did," Gianni said casually. "More than okay, in fact."

"What makes you so sure?" asked his niece. "You been in touch with him or something?"

"Not in decades. Until a couple days ago. When I found out he's hopin' to buy me outa my share of the restaurant and open up a gay bar."

"In Bloomfield Center?" said Pete.

"Bloomfield's come a long way since you left it, Peter," said his mother. "The whole world has. Maybe you've been too busy sitting naked in the hot tub to notice."

"I've noticed, I've noticed. But how did Freddy—"

"Well, it's a little complicated," Gianni explained, "but you remember I mentioned this guy Mort who handled all the business stuff for my old boss Paulie—"

"Yeah," said Pete. "Mort the liar from Paramus."

"Except it turns out he's not a liar, just very discreet. So it was on the hush-hush that, when Paulie died, Freddy got his share of things because he and Paulie had gotten let's say very close in Paulie's later years."

"Very close?" said Bert. "Like, how close?"

Gianni shrugged. "None a my business. And wit' due respect, Bert, none a yours either."

"Never stopped me before," the old man shot back. "But I mean, who wouldn't be curious if ya just found out the whole Mafia's breakin' gay?"

"Well, be that as it may," said Gianni, "Mort got me and Freddy onna phone together and we had kind of an amazing conversation. He apologized for what a schmuck he used to be. I told him how sorry I was about his son. We were both pretty choked up by the end, to tell the truth. Anyway, he made me an offer and I said I'd think about it."

Gertie had drained her glass and was in the process of refilling it, her heavy rings tinkling against the nearly empty bottle. Flushed with wine and excitement, she said, "Which brings us to a wonderful piece of news we want to share."

Something in those words seemed instantly to boost the humidity in the crowded room. Pete felt the itch that comes before a sweat beginning at his hairline.

"We were going to save it till we had the cheesecake," his mother went on, "but since it's sort of come up already…Well, you tell it, honey."

She nodded coquettishly at Gianni. He rearranged his booted foot, leaned forward in his armchair, and said, "Well, when I first came down here and bought this little place, I thought it'd just be for vacations till I retired, which I didn't think would be anytime soon. But wit' everything that was goin' on, I started thinkin' why wait? Why the hell wait? How many good years I got left? No one knows. And when those knuckleheads grabbed Gertie, well, that made me look it right innee eye how touch-and-go life is, how it could all go sour in a minute, how someone you love could vanish any day. I mean, it happens. So why wait to be happy? Anyway, that was my thinking, and then Freddy's offer came in, and me and Gertie talked it over. So I called Freddy back and, after we came to terms, he said he'd love to have me as a guest at his grand opening. I told him I'd be honored t'attend. Wit' clothes on. So that's it. It's a done deal, I'm retirin'. No more business hassles, no more Jersey winters."

He broke off for a sip of wine and raised his glass toward his blushing lover. "And what makes it all the sweeter," he went on, "is that my beautiful Gertie is plannin' to move in wit' me."

Pete heard himself say, "Here?"

Penelope kicked him underneath the coffee table.

"Of course here," Gertie said. "Where we have family."

Pete gulped some wine.

"Well, I think it's terrific," said Penelope.

"Thank you, hon," said Gertie. "And the best part is how easy it'll be to visit with you two. Without all the fuss and travel. Just casual. Make dinners. Meet on the beach. Not saying every day. Maybe three, four times a week. Won't need any planning. You know, just drop by."

"Just...drop by?" said Pete.

Penelope kicked him harder.

"Sure. Just spur of the moment. You know, coffee and a shmooze whenever. Just being together like a family. I think it'll be wonderful. Don't you?"

⚓ ⚓ ⚓

ABOUT THE AUTHOR

Laurence Shames is the author of seventeen *Key West Capers,* as well as many other works of fiction and nonfiction. As a ghostwriter, he has penned four *New York Times* bestsellers, in four different categories, under four different names. Formerly a columnist for *Esquire* and *The New York Observer,* he has contributed hundreds of articles and essays to publications including *Vanity Fair, Outside, Travel & Leisure,* and *The New York Times Magazine.* His work has been translated into more than a dozen languages, and he is a recipient of the United Kingdom's *Macallan Last Laugh Dagger* for his comic mystery writing.

To learn more, please visit https://laurenceshames.com

Works by Laurence Shames

Key West Capers–

Key West Normal

The Paradise Gig

Nacho Unleashed

One Big Joke

One Strange Date

Key West Luck

Tropical Swap

Shot on Location

The Naked Detective

Welcome to Paradise

Mangrove Squeeze

Virgin Heat

Tropical Depression

Sunburn

Scavenger Reef

Florida Straits

Key West Short Fiction–

Chickens

New York & California Novels–

Money Talks

The Angels' Share

Nonfiction–

The Hunger for More

The Big Time